Blood To Blood

Ifè Oshun

Second Edition

Papa Grace Publishing

ISBN-10: 0985923539

ISBN-13: 978-0-9859235-3-2

To my mother, Sybil.

Continue on your journey in Peace, Light and Love

and remember

"There's no such thing as can't."

CONTENTS
♫♪♫

1. MOM'S GONNA KILL ME

The Change was starting.

A tingle coursed through my veins like the first flutterings of a new butterfly's wings, and I distinctly heard the heartbeats of everyone in the room.

Part of me was excited. After all, I'd soon be full-grown Shimshana. But then another part was scared... How exactly would The Change affect me? More importantly, would I still be able to sing afterwards?

The tingling faded into the background, though, as I watched the number of comments explode. *Mom's gonna kill me*, I thought.

We (Kat Trio) were about to sign our very first album deal, and somehow word had already gotten out on Facebook. Pivoting the laptop on the table's smooth surface, I showed my profile page to the others in the sun-filled conference room.

My group mates, Julietta and LaLa; our manager, Nina; and the label's A&R Director—um, was his name Raj?—were too preoccupied to look up.

"Seven hundred and eighty-four friend requests," I said. My mouth was suddenly parched, despite the lemon wedge I'd been sucking.

LaLa mumbled something undecipherable while painstakingly inscribing lyrics on her striped sleeve. Julietta popped bubblegum and barely looked up from texting one of her boyfriends. "A step up from the nine friends you have now," she quipped.

Raj smiled and passed Nina copies of the contract. "Might as well get used to it, ladies," he responded in his smooth London/East Indian accent. At that moment, he reminded me of an antsy Las Vegas dealer. You know, the type you see in the movies; twitching right before someone at the blackjack table is dragged into the backroom to get beat down for cheating the house. Or maybe the twitch I thought I saw in his grin was just a projection of my own guilt. After all, I was the one cheating the house. I was breaking my family's number one, all-time rule: stay low-profile. And I was the one who was lying. I gulped down what felt like a cotton ball forming in my throat.

Nina finally looked up from signing the contracts. "Your turn," she said to us. "Just print your names." Pens began signing, and papers glided like flattened sharks back and forth across the table amidst a sea of water bottles, cough drops, and hot cups of tea until all the lines were signed. The contracts' final destination was the notary public at the end of the table who verified the info and stamped them with her seal. Nina and Raj shook hands before she turned and spread her manicured fingers toward us. "Congrats, girls," she said. "You've just signed a deal with House Quake."

I didn't know whether to laugh, cry, or scream, and obviously, neither did Jules and LaLa. Despite just getting what we had worked for and dreamed of for the past three years, we sat mutely for a moment, staring at one another in the wake of Nina's words.

None of us girls had typical sixteen year-old lives. Instead of fashion, boys, and reality TV we had writing, rehearsing, and performing wherever we could. Talent shows, festivals, and church were the only dates we had, and over the past year, any gig that I could sneak behind my parents' backs was another notch in our collective belt. We were on a mission. We wanted to do this as a career. And everybody knew that in order to make it, you had to grab all the opportunities you could while you were still young. In my case, my life was even less typical and there was no point in waiting. Singing was my heart, my soul, and my waking dream. It was the only thing I could ever imagine doing. Forever.

Kat Trio was a hobby until we met Nina, who told us she could take us far if we were serious. Soon, we entered and won NE Rising Stars, an annual showcase of the best talent from across the Northeast. The prize package (photo shoot, demo CD, and potential signing with a mid-sized record company) was so publicized, my parents refused to allow me to interview with the label. They even made me promise to stop performing. I lied and told them I would.

I apologized to the girls, telling them that I couldn't meet with the label because Mom and Dad wanted me to focus on my double English classes at school. Not a *total* lie, since my parents are really big on education. Between the two of them, they have hundreds of degrees in almost as many languages and or dialects, gathering dust in a secret room in the basement. But to be completely honest, my parents were definitively against *any* member of the family being in the public spotlight. Even if it was the only yet-to-turn-immortal member. Me. Our peaceful existence depended on the ability to blend into the mortal world. Attracting national attention to myself would defeat the "blending mandate," so this record deal and sudden fame stuff was a serious no-no.

Even worse, Mom and Dad didn't know that I'd broken my promise and was still doing gigs. Every night the girls and I spent gigging was a night when my parents thought I was studying at either LaLa or Jules' house. Now the record deal would expose me as a scheming traitor, and I was sure not even The Change and the immortality it would bring could save me from Mom's wrath.

And if (a very big if) Mom didn't kill me once the truth came out, she would surely incinerate me into a small gray mound of breathable dust after I gathered up the guts to tell her and Dad that I was considering dropping out of high school to make an album.

So instead of laughing, crying or even screaming, I just sat there, pen still in my hand—slack-jawed with the realization the contract I'd just signed was really my own death warrant.

2. REFLECTION

Julietta snapped me out of my stupor. "Still haven't told your parents, huh?" she whispered conspiratorially after a quick peek at Nina. Our manager didn't know the "parental" signature on my contract was forged.

I felt the urge to run like heck. "Bathroom," I answered.

Once there, I checked out my reflection in the large vanity mirror and wished I would change into an immortal before breaking the news to the family later on that night. I was still in the vulnerable part of my existence— childhood—but my pending maturity might give me a chance at surviving Mom's red rage.

Immortal kids are identical to mortal kids when it comes to physical development. Then somewhere between the ages of sixteen to eighteen, our aging slows (and according to Mom, eventually stops about a thousand years later) as our immortality, complete with unique abilities, personality, blah, blah, blah come online.

Would The Change make my face look different? My eyes were a brighter brown than usual (but that probably was from the excitement of the record deal), and underneath the surface of my skin (my sister calls it "flawless milk chocolate") the blood rushed and gave me the usual mortal flush. My hair looked the same, too: a barely controlled mass. Today, I'd managed to weave it into a single braid that swung between my shoulder blades. The T-shirt, jeans, and pink suede boots fit the way they did the day before.

So, okay, I looked the same. But I didn't *feel* the same. Something was different. "Your dream's coming true," I told my reflection. "Why can't you just relax for once and enjoy this?" I held my breath. And waited.

As usual, after a moment of silence, my reflection took on a life of its own. It peered from one side of the mirror to the other as if making sure we were alone. I giggled and wondered for the millionth time what the girls would think if they ever saw this.

Reflection, hands on hips, glared at me. "You can't relax because you're a dumbass."

Before I could shoot back a retort, the bathroom door flew open and in walked a no-nonsense-looking exec type. "Hi!" I blurted, praying she wouldn't spot my errant image in the mirror. Luckily, she looked at me like I was a nutcase and headed straight into a stall.

Exhaling, I snapped my fingers once and Reflection immediately reverted back to an ordinary...reflection. A reflection of a liar, nervously chewing her inner cheek and going against everything her parents taught her.

Back in the conference room, Raj was gone and Julietta was doing a seated happy dance in her chair. Magenta-colored hair and gold hoop earrings bounced around her face. "Girl, guess what's happening!" she squealed. She stood up to do her signature step: two quick steps to the right, two to the left, small hop forward, finish with outstretched jazz hands. "Starving Artists just canceled their gig at the Garden." Her fingers still danced in the air. "We might be able to squeeze in there before the other opening acts and do a song!"

Starving Artists was voted one of the "Ones To Watch" in *Frunt* magazine's highly touted year-end issue. They were slated to open for international superstar Charmain, whose single "Tell It Like It Was" was number one on the chart for the eighth week in a row and breaking all kinds of download sales records.

"Why would they cancel?" I wondered aloud.

LaLa scratched her head under her Red Sox cap. "Girl, who cares," she said. "We are sooo in. You know Nina never tells us anything until she's almost one hundred percent sure." Her eyebrows threatened to mate with her hairline as she cocked her head in our manager's direction. "She's on the phone with them right now."

Sure enough, Nina, pressed into a corner of the room, spoke urgently into her cell. My stomach flipped with excitement. This was really happening.

"And if that weren't enough," Julietta gushed, "we'll be working with—OMG—Sawyer Creed!"

My smile immediately crashed and burned. "The dude who did that Swedish Moreno track? The one that sounds like it was made with a toy keyboard?"

"Duh, Angel." Jules rolled her eyes. "Only the number one track of the year!"

It may have been number one, but to me the tune was one step above a nursery rhyme. For the millionth time, I wondered how the most simple-minded songs became huge hits and figured it had something to do with the limitations of mortal hearing. Nevertheless, I swallowed my criticism. "If you have nothing nice to say..." Dad always told us.

Eventually, Nina, taking note of the silence and what was probably my dubious expression, set her Blackberry down. "Raj followed you for months," she said to me. "Trust me, he's a fan. And he thinks the natural match for your work is Sawyer."

The skepticism I felt etched on my face was now echoed on LaLa's. "They say he's got a bad temper," she said. "You really think this is a good idea?"

With determination, Nina quickly punched laptop keys and pulled up a *Billboard.com* feature titled:

"Pop's Teen Genius"

"Creed's the future," she asserted while we scanned the article. His rugged, unsmiling face hosted piercingly green eyes, which seemed to hover in front of the halo of his blond shoulder-length hair.

"Yikes," Julietta said, "he's hot."

Nina ignored the interjection. "He's riding the wave from that Moreno track. The timing's right and, as I understand, he's got stacks and stacks of tracks. I smell a hit."

The ticking of the huge clock on the wall seemed very loud to me as I swiveled my chair around to gaze out the wall of glass overlooking the Boston skyline. Something didn't feel right. My eyes were focused on the way the afternoon sun glinted off the tops of cars in the traffic stream below. "Is he the only producer we're slated to work with?" I asked. Nina's heartbeat accelerated slightly. Not good.

"That's something we need to discuss." Nina pressed the tips of her fingers together until her hands formed a triangle. "You didn't sign a record deal, per se. What we agreed to was recording one song."

"What! Only one song?" The words came out in what felt like a growl as the cars, the sunlight, and the skyline disappeared from my view. For a split second, I was one hundred percent my mother's daughter. I saw nothing but red. Angry, bloody red.

3. A MILLION TINY PIECES

Julietta took a step away from me and LaLa slid to the edge of her seat in the opposite direction. Nina's heart rate speeded up some more, but she stayed put, her poker face never flinching as my eyes met hers. I kept my voice level and calm. "We have an album's worth of material. At least forty-five songs."

"Labels are unwilling to put a lot of money into new acts these days." Nina's voice took on the annoyingly soothing tone she reserved for less-than-ideal situations. "Once you prove yourself with a track that has downloading and or ringtones heat, I'll be empowered to go ahead and negotiate another contract."

So in other words, everything was riding on hitting the Top 10 with just one measly tune produced by the hotheaded Sawyer Creed. Did I really just throw my family's traditions under the bus for the sake of *one song*? Inside of me, an icky tide of resentment rose toward Creed.

It was illogical, seeing as he had nothing to do with the decision I'd made to go against my family's wishes, or the fact that I didn't read the contract before signing it. But logic didn't matter. At that moment, Creed represented all that was wrong with the music industry and I was going to hate him anyway.

LaLa, fanning herself, responded first. "Don't worry. I'm in." Julietta, swiping sweat from her forehead, nodded in agreement. They both glanced expectantly at me. I nodded.

"Good," Nina said as she lifted her bone-straight weave off the nape of her neck in an attempt to cool down. "Raj went to get him."

"He's coming up here?" Julietta said excitedly.

"Now?" My voice sounded like a squeak.

"His studio's just around the corner," Nina answered as LaLa's head swiveled between the three of us.

Heavens to leotards, it just kept getting worse and worse.

As if on cue, the door opened and in strutted a triumphant-looking Raj followed by…Sawyer Creed. The latter seemed annoyed, and his dark eyebrows were drawn together in a unibrow-inducing frown. He looked the way I felt: ticked off.

"Ladies, meet our resident genius, Sawyer." Raj— slight, dark, roughly five-foot-seven—was the exact opposite of Sawyer, who stood at what looked like six-foot-four with an athletic build. Julietta immediately jumped up to shake his hand and LaLa and I rolled our eyes at her never-ending boy craziness. Raj continued the intros throughout the endless handshaking before everybody finally sat down.

"Again, welcome to the mill, girls," Raj said before shooting me a sheepish smile. "Not to say we'll be grinding you up, but you'll be grinding even more." He beamed,

11

seemingly pleased with his use of '90s American slang. Sawyer sat sullen, silent and unimpressed. "Sawyer," Raj continued, "Kat Trio have crazy potential, and I'm confident that together you'll come up with a slamming number one."

Four sets of eyes turned toward Sawyer.

His skin was somewhat pale and his hair, almost as long as mine, was pulled back to reveal a square jawline. His Atlanta Braves baseball cap rested on the table next to a pair of black Ray Bans; unusual since most of the industry dudes, at least the ones we'd met, hid underneath caps pulled down as low as possible over black shades and never bothered to remove either whether they were indoors or out.

He sported a midnight-blue tracksuit with gold piping and his goatee was kind of fuzzy, as if he'd been in the studio for the past month and was now stepping out to forage for food. I remembered the article mentioned that he'd produced almost a dozen Top 20 songs before he hit the age of seventeen a little over a year ago. "Incredible Green Eyes" struck me as a cool song title just as his gaze shifted to mine. His frown deepened. Hmm...he wasn't annoyed; he was concentrating on something. I wondered what... Oops, I was staring at him. Awkward. Mentally insert foot in mouth. Now, tear gaze away...

"Sawyer usually doesn't leave the studio," Raj continued. "Had to drag him out. Maybe you guys can all get together tomorrow?" He and Nina quickly made arrangements for our first session before I ran off to my after-school tutoring job.

# # #

Later, while picking up candy wrappers and rearranging the chairs in the empty middle-school classroom where I'd just finished tutoring, I wondered why Mom and Dad insisted I have a job. I was ahead in completing credits for the year, and as a result, my school day ended earlier. But the job was slightly annoying mainly because one of the sixth graders had a crush on me. He always got red in the face when I stood next to him and stammered when I asked him questions. Chuckling, I picked up another wrapper, and remembered how lame life was when I was in sixth grade, before I started singing and before I stopped caring about what the other kids thought of me. Now school didn't matter at all, and stuff like being popular and the upcoming prom were just a distraction from what really mattered: music.

I grabbed my boots from the corner where they lay drying. They'd gotten soaked when I'd stepped in a slush puddle earlier, and instead of tracking water through the room I'd changed into my track shoes. *Thank goodness I decided to bring them home for washday,* I thought as I took the sneakers off and stuffed them back into my knapsack.

My cell blared "Madame Butterfly" and Julietta's smiling face popped up on the screen. "What's up?" I asked.

"Girl, we're doing the Garden!" Jules was the group's broadcaster of good news, and the ever-conservative Nina used that enthusiasm to save time by making one phone call instead of three.

"Wow. That's over fourteen thousand people!"

"Yep! So...you're, like, telling your folks tonight, right?"

"Yeah." Ultimate resign. "Guess so."

Jules was my best mortal friend, which meant I could tell her everything... except the truth about my family or my pending immortality. Unlike me, she was optimistic.

Maybe it was because her mom was super-supportive of her singing in our group. I envied that support. How cool would it be if, after I told them the truth, Mom and Dad came to the Garden gig? But then again, they'd probably question my sanity. After all, why would I put our way of life in jeopardy for a chance to have my voice heard by mortals if I weren't insane?

"LaLa and I can come over if you need us," Julietta was saying. "You know. Moral support."

LaLa and Julietta had been over to the house many times for sleepovers, homework, and writing sessions, but they had no idea my family was immortal and would probably die of fright if they saw Mom's Shimshana reaction to my news.

"Thanks, girl. I think I'll be okay though. Maybe you guys can come over tomorrow to scrape what's left of me off the wall."

Unaware I was serious, Julietta laughed. "Okay, girl, we'll be there." She clicked off.

A movement caught the corner of my eye. Glimmering in one of the classroom's large windows was Reflection. She was staring at me, but I hadn't given the usual mental permission that allowed her to take on a life of her own.

"I didn't call you!" I exclaimed.

"You don't have to. Now, what was I saying before? Oh yeah, you're a nut job, attention-freak, doofus."

I squeezed my eyes shut and concentrated, but she was still there, smirking, when I opened them. This couldn't be happening. Even worse, what if Reflection was right?

What if all the attention from Quake and the Garden gig ended up hurting my family by exposing our true nature? I anxiously paced while imagining the online media blitz; the posts and tweets about the Beacon Hill mom, *my* mom, who drank the blood of willing donors.

I felt Reflection's eyes following me as I agonized. "Hmph," she said, "Jules isn't the only one who thinks the blond dude's hot, huh? Mom's really gonna kill—"

"Enough!" I yelled. I glanced at the window and Reflection was gone. Sigh of relief. Then I heard the front door open. I turned to see her there, three-dimensional and with a hand on the doorknob.

I nearly screamed.

"You have no control—actually, you never had any control over me," she said in a quiet, matter-of-fact voice. "I'm leaving now. It's really for the best." Reflection started changing then. Her skin became a more golden shade of brown. The length of her hair shrunk and got curlier. Her body grew rounder and fuller in certain places...

"What do you think you're doing?" I said through my teeth. "Get back in that window now!"

But all she did was peer at me with a weird little smile, as if her upper lip was partially stuck to her front teeth, before waving her hand goodbye and softly closing the door behind her.

Racing to the door, I flung it open and scanned the hallway. No one was there. I slammed the door shut, leaned against it, and exhaled. My stomach felt like it had broken into a million tiny pieces, and each little shard of what used to be my lucidity floated around my insides like tiny islands of foreboding. Sweat broke out everywhere I had skin; and my hands shook like they belonged on someone else's body. I remembered I hadn't slept for almost two days. I tried to breathe, deep and slowly the way Dad taught me to do when I felt like this; like I, and the world, were both falling apart. His technique didn't quite work this time.

I need Mr. C., I thought.

With an overwhelming need to escape whatever doom I just *knew* was gearing up to steamroll me flatter than an oil stain in the middle of the street, I snatched my keys, cell, and knapsack, and ran out of that room like a bat out of you know where.

4. MUSIC

Outside, snow drifted down in fat flakes that stuck to my hair and nose as I sprinted through rush hour Harvard Square traffic to catch a taxi.

Inside the cab, the driver flashed me a puzzled look before I gave him the address to the studio of my singing coach, former international concert pianist Sheridan Caulkins, and a.k.a., "Mr. C." The cab driver shot me more weird eye action before finally pulling away from the curb. *What's his problem?* I wondered, looking down at myself for an answer only to realize, with a gasp, the reason for the guy's behavior.

I'd just run through the snow barefoot. But the forgotten boots didn't trouble me as much as the fact that my feet were warm and dry.

I decided to fix it with a glamour—a spell designed to make things appear anyway you want them to. Dad, who's like a guru of illusion, taught me how, but I could never be as good as he is. Dad can make himself, or any of us, look like any race or even gender we want. It's his ability to conjure up radical illusions that make him and Mom look, to mortal eyes, as if they're aging (a pretty handy skill to have, since our family's lived in the same Beacon Hill brownstone since the early 1800s). I quickly performed a simple glamour for "shoe" that would have made Dad proud. "Shoes," I whispered to seal the spell into place.

By the time the cab arrived at the rehearsal studio, I could barely breathe with all the anticipation. It had been five weeks since my last session, and during that time I hadn't known how much I missed the place until I pushed through the squeaky metal door.

Mr. C. was sitting at his polished grand piano, finishing up with another client. I sat down in the corner to wait. Soon, he gave me the kind of firm hug a grandfather would. "Congratulations on the contract, my dear. The first of many I'm sure." His hawk-like eyes took in my appearance from head to toe. "You've been sleeping less," he said, before his gaze stopped at my feet. "Interesting," he mused.

Mr. C. sometimes didn't act like a normal mortal. I was positive my glamour for "shoe" worked perfectly, because no one looked at me sideways since I got out of the cab. But Caulkins' gaze, zoned in on my feet, was accompanied by his signature "enigma stare"—a peculiar set of his face that never gave away anything of what he observed.

"I'm sorry. I've been away too long," I replied.

"You've been performing so much, you may not even need me for practice anymore." He winked at me before lowering himself onto the bench to pound out a scale in the key of C.

The stupid, the scary, and the confusing immediately evaporated as I reveled in the cleansing act of breathing in, letting my breath slowly flow back out through my diaphragm and lungs, and expressing my jumbled emotions with *just the right* sound; using breath, throat, gut, and tongue to form aural bubbles through lips and teeth. It was these times, during the execution of song, when I felt complete. Normal. My voice caressed high C as I watched the sound waves flow from my mouth…

Mr. C. once said he thought my octave range was well above fifteen. We both knew this was allegedly humanly impossible…and he never mentioned it again. He always made me feel like he had my back, like he completely accepted me, even though he didn't completely *understand* me.

We climbed higher along the scale ladder until he reached the end. "How about a song," he suggested with that twinkle in his eye.

"O Mio Babbino Caro!" I squealed before his knotted hands delicately introduced the first chord. Bubblegum pop lyrics were what I belted out on stage, but my first love was opera. Only my family and Mr. C. knew that. To me, its soaring arias were the closest thing to aural perfection known to mortal or immortal. For the longest time, I thought everyone also saw musical notes the same way I did; as rays of light before my eyes—some darker than others and some as bright as a quasar—that danced together in rhythm with the melody. Beyond the light show, Mr. C. arched over the grand, his nicotine-stained fingers hung in mid-air before dropping forcefully on the keys. Pushing out the highest note in the song, and climbing from there, I emitted the note-for-which-there-was-no-name and watched the light rays bend…

And then, Mr. C's eyes bulged like they'd pop out of his skull, right before he crumpled to a dead slump all over the piano keys.

5. DECISION

I yelled his name, but there was no response. He had a pulse, his chest rose up and down, but for once Mr. C. looked every one of his seventy-seven mortal years. His eyes fluttered opened as he slowly raised himself into a sitting position.

I reached for his water glass. He glanced around the room as if he didn't know where he was and, with shaky hands, gripped the glass, emptied it, and handed it back to me.

"What happened?"

Was that accusation in his voice? No, of course not, I thought. I was nowhere near him when he passed out. So why *did* I feel guilty? I placed the empty glass back on the piano. "You passed out, Mr. C. How do you feel?"

"I'm fine, girl, fine," he replied brusquely while stubbornly straightening his back and ancient tie.

"Mr. C—" I cut myself off because I didn't know what to say. Would I say sorry? Sorry for what? Could I confide in him? Say I was scared of getting massacred by my Shimshana Mom before I had the chance to morph into an immortal?

He stared at me but his gaze seemed off-center. "You seem different," he said, "in a way I was unable to name earlier, but can now. Innocence is disappearing from your face." I hated when he said weirdo fortune-teller type stuff like this. His eyes were now refocused and bore into me. "Keep telling yourself why you want to sing, Angel. Keep telling them who you really are."

#

I contemplated his words later, before getting out of the taxi and forcing my feet to walk down the narrow, brick streets toward home. Despite the fainting incident, Mr. C. had refused to stop our session. As a result, I felt strong enough, calm enough, to go home and face Mom's killing wrath. The straps of my overloaded knapsack dug into my shoulder as I took in my surroundings with the heightened awareness of a death-row prisoner making that final trek to the electric chair. Ironic. I felt like a dead girl walking, but was probably now, or soon to be, immortal.

I let my mind roam while breathing in the crisp winter air. The feeling of my toes catching in the crevices between the uneven bricks made me appreciate, again, the history of my neighborhood. The gas lighting, colonial architecture, and sense of danger in the dark, centuries-old alleyways always fascinated me. Again, I imagined what it was like when Mom and Dad first moved here masquerading as British white people.

Adopting the common name of Brown, Dad posed as a wealthy tea merchant with abolitionist tendencies. He built his Beacon Hill brownstone mansion, where he settled with his genteel wife (Mom—ha!) and several people that everyone thought were freed slaves who worked for him as servants, but were actually my older sisters and brothers who came and went through the years. After a couple decades, Mom and Dad were safer in their own skin, literally, since a number of affluent African-Americans had established residences, schools, and churches on the Hill. They emerged as a young couple with a baby girl (my sister Cecilia, or Cici for short) whose parents had allegedly worked at the estate and bought it once the Brit merchant and his childless wife "died."

For the next one hundred and seventy years, my family masqueraded as their own descendants so we could live a normal life among the cobblestones. Through the 1900s, Mom and Dad went back to school. Again. This time, she studied "modern" U.S. law while he studied Western medicine, both adding to that massive pile of diplomas, writs, and papyrus. Dad says his "new" knowledge of mortal anatomy, and his practice at Beth Israel, helps him conjure up solid, long-term age glamours.

And, as Dad predicted almost two centuries ago, this neighborhood was the perfect choice for them. The Massachusetts Historical Preservation Society protects the surrounding buildings, and as a result, the neighborhood's suspended in a time bubble, with virtually no new construction. Despite the modern indoor conveniences of electric light, Wi-Fi, and dish TV, non-resident parking was almost non-existent and there wasn't a vacant lot to be seen. Modern-day Beacon Hill was not only charming, it was perfect for a family of immortals. And it was perfect for me.

My feet came to a stop. I was home. I rocked back on my heels to peer up at the blood-red door at the top of the flight of steep, wide steps.

In the midst of climbing up, I stopped and listened. Mom was in the kitchen, humming an old Beatles song, probably cooking dinner for me and Dad, since we were the only ones in the house who ate mortal food. I took a deep breath and wondered what tonight's announcement would do to my relationship with my parents. It was a betrayal, but it was necessary. Sighing, I turned the key in the lock and reached for the doorknob. I stopped. Dang it, I grumbled, I nearly forgot about shielding my thoughts from Dad and Cici before going inside.

Steadying myself, I visualized a haze fixing itself around my mind, shielding my thoughts from the pull of their telepathic abilities.

Alrighty then, it was now or never. My heartbeat kicked up a few notches. The thought of them hearing me out here, agonizing over the revelation of my upcoming bombshell, filled me with panic. Drat, I was supposed to stay calm.

I nervously grasped the doorknob. But my hand kept going, through the knob and through the door itself as if neither were there. "Whoa…" I'd never done that before. Was I immortal now? This *was* something I'd seen Mom do millions of times…

Wow, I was immortal! Wait a minute… Oh no! I was turning into Mom! I drew my hand back and flexed the fingers. Was I supposed to understand anything that was happening to me anymore? I stuck my hand back through the door. "Cool…" At least I didn't have to worry about Mom killing me anymore…did I? I steeled myself.

Well, I'll never be the same. So, I'll make a new kind of entrance, I thought.

With determination, I took another deep breath and proceeded to step, literally, through the door.

6. MEET THE PARENTS

As I pushed my left arm, shoulder, and foot through the door, a strong hand grabbed me from the other side and yanked. Before I could blink, I was standing inside the foyer facing Mom.

"Angelica Isis Clarissa Brown, what on earth do you think you are doing?"

Mom, wearing a red holiday apron decorated with a huge smiling turkey, looked the equivalent of twenty-eight mortal years. We shared the same medium brown coloring and height, but unlike mine, her hair was flat-ironed and shaped into a nifty bob, kind of like the hairstyles seen on the figures of men and women painted on ancient Egyptian structures. Made sense, since she was born in Alexandria, Egypt somewhere around 12 B.C.

"I just had to sort your molecules so you would not get stuck halfway in the door," she lectured. "What would the neighbors think if they saw that? And where are your shoes?" She kissed my forehead and hugged me close. Tonight her cat-like eyes were the color of toffee and, as always, had the intensity of laser beams.

"Mom, I have something important I need to say. To the whole family." No need beating around the bush. And I wasn't sure how long I could keep up the shield before passing out from exhaustion.

Mom's eyes narrowed and swept me from head to toe. She was scanning me. Great. "The Change," she said. "It is commencing. And you are shielding. What do you want to hide?"

At that moment, Cecilia swooshed in. "Howdy Angel. Oh, you're shielding. Hmmm...family conference?"

Mute nod.

"I'll get Dad," she said before flying, literally, up the stairs. After a cryptic glance at me, Mom disappeared, not literally, into the kitchen.

I hung my coat up in the coat closet, right beside the small hook placed there by Mom for Dad. He was notorious for losing his keys, and I smiled, remembering his multitude of mad stomps through the house searching for them while stubbornly refusing to use magic to find them.

I ran my hand along the two-foot tall iron sculpture of a goddess—a family heirloom created by granddaddy around 1000 B.C.—as I made my way to our official "conference room," the dining room. The clattering of plates and other cooking sounds from the kitchen suddenly made me feel so hungry I could eat my hand. But when I inhaled the aroma, I almost puked my intestines (the only thing in my stomach). Did this mean the blood-drinking part of The Change had kicked in?

I turned into the dining room and tossed my bag onto an altar Dad had carved back in 17th century China. Falling into one of the sturdy chairs surrounding the mahogany table, I stretched my legs out in front of me and reveled in the warm smells of orange oil furniture polish, incense, and fresh flowers.

It was wicked good to be home.

Mom entered with the food. "Did you eat anything today, honey?" I shook my head, but hesitated over the oven-baked potatoes, grilled chicken breast, and string beans. She gestured to two pitchers. "Drink?"

"Milk." I watched her pour it into one of the glasses she'd brought. Picking up the second pitcher, she filled half of a glass with blood for herself. I sniffed and wrinkled my nose.

"Try?" she asked.

"Ewww."

"You have to eat something, dear."

I started picking at the beans. "Type A?" I inquired, glancing at her glass.

"Yes, a new donor." A really long time ago, Mom stopped ravishing mortals for moral reasons and now had donors, willing mortals who offered their blood as food. The pitcher's label read "SEBASTIAN." She put the glass under her nose and inhaled deeply. "He is Brazilian. He has a fabulous, nutty taste. With a hint of citrus."

Dad moved down the stairs. No doubt Mom had sent him mental images of everything that had happened since she'd pulled me through the door. "Do I hear my little honey bear hiding her thoughts from me?" he called out in a booming voice.

At six-foot-eight, Dad filled most rooms he stood in, which is why he built the house with uncharacteristically tall ceilings. Bald and dark brown with a wiry build and sculpted beard, Dad had an easy-going nature. Who'd a thunk that, one; he'd been born in ancient Kush circa 250 A.D., or, two; he was a wizard with a craft so epic he could level an entire city with a few incantations.

"Hey Dad." I didn't allow him to bear-hug me into his arms as usual, but remained in my seat, concentrating on keeping my shield intact.

Dad doesn't technically read minds. Rather, thoughts are drawn to him as if they're metal shavings and he's a magnet. Cici has the same ability. My effort was focused on stopping my thoughts (easy prey because they concerned the family's well-being) from attaching to Dad and my sister. I could feel my face scrunched up with concentration. He exchanged an "our baby's growing up" look with Mom before sitting down.

Cici flitted in and sat down in the most neutral position she could find, making sure she was facing everyone equally. At one hundred sixty-seven years old, she was my closest sibling in age and looked the mortal equivalent of twenty.

Tall and dark chocolate like Dad, she had the physique of a model. She'd recently dyed and cut her waist-length hair, and it now lay blond and close to her scalp in a face-framing style that emphasized her glittering, reddish-brown eyes and the high cheekbones we both inherited from Mom. Her new haircut was kind of butch, but it was balanced by the girly gear she liked to wear.

I missed braiding Cici's hair, missed how she would sit between my knees while my fingers flitted through her locks and experimented with different patterns while we talked about everything under the sun.

She was my only true confidant.

There was a time when we had no secrets, even after I, at the age of twelve, had asked her and Dad to not read my thoughts. When they complied, I felt free to share with her every bad thing I wanted to hide from our parents.

Shortly after that, Cici informed me that she had constructed a special place in her mind for all of my "adventures," away from Dad's unintentional prying. That so earned her forever points.

But now, I avoided her eyes. Ever since I'd decided to be serious about music, I'd kept it secret from her for fear Dad may find out and blame her as an accomplice. No need for her to go down in Mom's flames with me.

As still as sighted stones, my family watched me chew anxiously on the tines of my dinner fork. Finally, I took a deep breath. "Mom, Dad. Kat Trio got a record deal. I'm dropping out of school."

Stunned silence. Cici glanced nervously at Mom, who, from the look on her reddening face, had begun her bloody thoughts. Right then, I knew I was dead meat.

7. THE BABY'S GROWING UP

Despite Mom's growing rage, I quickly plowed ahead…while I still *had* a head. "I will pursue a recording career. I will go on tour. I will play the Garden. I want to make records. Move into my own place. And sing on TV, videos, and the radio."

Cici grinned. Dad frowned. And Mom literally saw red. The room took on her bad mood by turning a slight shade of burgundy and gaining a few degrees in temperature. Typical Shimshana anger stuff.

I retained a cool façade. I was prepared for this.

"What did you say?" Mom said in that certain tone.

"I want to—" I started to repeat myself word for word.

"Have you forgotten your Mahá, Angelica?" she interrupted tersely.

Mahá was the coming-out party for new immortals, which lasted for days. It happened immediately after The Change and was one of the most important events in an immortal's existence. Other immortals from everywhere came to meet and observe the "New One." Mahá was as old as the oldest of us and there was no getting out of it.

"No," I answered, deflated. Spent, I released my shield, wanting nothing more than to climb into bed and try to go to sleep.

"Why, Angel? Why do you feel the need to do this...pop star thing?" she asked.

"School sucks. I want to sing."

"You want to sing for mortals," Dad said.

"I want to sing for everybody."

He leaned forward, and extended the first two fingers of his left hand. "May I?" he inquired gently.

I paused for a second, and then nodded. He touched my temple. After a few seconds, he quickly pulled back and, after a brief pause, patted me on the shoulder. "I see it," he said. "You want to change the world into a better place with the music in your soul. You want to touch the hearts of people."

"Yeah, what you said, Dad."

Mom softened up and the burgundy disappeared. "Angel," she said." You are beginning to mature. Surely you see that now?" I nodded. "You most certainly will be Shimshana; it is in your blood. And those mortals you want to sing for and be with so badly will suddenly be food to you."

Dumbfounded, I looked to Dad.

"It is difficult, honey, when you are newborn Shimshana," he agreed. "Your natural tendency will be to...hunt." The word hung in the air like a threat. "You may not be able to... control yourself the way your mother and sister do."

"You mean I could..." the words stuck in my throat before rushing out in a blurt, "...want to kill Jules and LaLa?"

My eyes darted to Cici, who stared at the table. I eyed her with growing horror. "Cici? You didn't…?"

She eventually met my eyes. "It's almost impossible to stop. Mortals smell good, the way a roasted chicken still smells to you. It took me roughly fifty years before I got to the point where I didn't want, or need, to attack them." She quickly looked back down at the table.

"It is nothing to be ashamed of," Dad said. "It is your nature."

"We make the moral choice to find alternatives to hunting," Mom added, "but at our core we are hunters. Your band mates, your fans, your teachers, are all fleeting. We are immortal. We cannot afford to see life the way they do."

Tears dripped over my lower eyelashes as I fought the mental image of killing my best friends for food. But it wasn't the thought that made me cry. It was the knowledge that, despite the risk, I wasn't going to stop. "I'm still going to do what I said I'd do," I said.

Dad, looking slightly disgusted, shook his head. The room grew red and hot again. "Oooh, this child," Mom said from between clenched teeth.

"Let us talk, my love," Dad said, rising from the table and reaching for her hand.

She immediately focused on his eyes, took a deep breath, and clasped his hand. "We are not done with you, young lady," she said, never taking her eyes away from Dad's. "Wait here."

"Um, okay."

Clasping hands, Dad and Mom faced each other. She kissed the space between his bushy eyebrows and the two of them disappeared.

I whipped around to Cici. "D'you see where they're going this time?"

"Taj Mahál. She must be wicked mad."

I paced the floor as Cici floated near her chair. "They're going to keep treating me like a child," I complained.

"Hate to tell you this, Bighead, but you are a child. You're still mortal. And you've got no idea what you're in for."

Before I could ask her what she meant by that, Mom and Dad appeared in the same spot they vanished from. "One hour and twenty-seven minutes," Mom announced. Since she was able to teleport by collapsing space and time, she always told us how long it took to come to a decision as a way to communicate the gravity of the situation and the amount of thought that went into its resolution. Anything over an hour was bad news.

I looked at them expectantly. Cici eyeballed them for a second before pressing her lips together in what looked like disapproval.

"You have our blessing," Dad told me.

Confused, I glanced at Cici and her frown. This was good news, wasn't it? "Don't understand..." I said warily.

"We have one condition," Dad continued.

Uh, oh...

"We need to be locked to you at all times," said Mom.

"A mind lock! DAD!" A mind lock was a total abdication of privacy. Dad would be able to virtually go everywhere I went and see everything I saw, and even scarier, hear my thoughts twenty-four-seven. It was like Big Brother in your cranium. But worse.

Cici stared at the table again. I felt waves of panic. "Angel. Look at me. Take a deep breath," Mom said. "Put your feet back on the floor."

My panic had lifted me inches off the hardwood. Cici gasped in shock. "Since when do you levitate?"

"N-never! I mean since now!" I didn't even know how to get down. Fresh waves of panic started as I pushed helplessly against the ceiling. Would the bizarro-ness of this day never end? "Mom, help!" I pleaded.

She focused her gaze on the space beneath my feet, and I touched down.

"Angel," Dad said. "You must know we will not invade your privacy. Of course we will filter out...certain personal things. We need to stay connected because you are starting to shift. We need to know when things like this," he gestured toward my feet, "circumstances you may not be able to control, happen."

"Honey, soon you will have your Mahá," Mom said. "You would have to take some time off anyway, so if you feel you want to leave school a little earlier, we are okay with that. We can hire a tutor, and you can always go back to school." Her eyes glanced toward the part of the dining room floor above her and Dad's stash of diplomas. "The most important thing," she continued, "is safety."

"Aren't you afraid I'll blow our cover? That me being in the spotlight would expose us all?"

My parents exchanged a glance. Quick unspoken words passed from Dad to Cici, who crossed her arms. I cleared my throat, feeling left out of the silent conversation.

"We had that concern when you were younger," Mom said, "but now we can see that you understand how important it is that we remain, at least in the eyes of the mortal world, normal."

"We know you will never do anything to intentionally damage our life here," Dad added before casting another quick glance at Cici and giving an almost imperceptible nod.

"I've been lying to you all," I confessed and sighed in resignation. "I never stopped performing. I just couldn't stop singing." More tears.

"I know," Mom said tightly. I was thrown off by the calmness she displayed at my admission of guilt. She gently lifted my chin and wiped my tears away with a dinner napkin. "We want you to be happy," she continued. "If singing on some stage somewhere is what makes you happy, so be it. You would not be the first immortal to do so."

I exhaled in relief.

"But you cannot fool yourself," Dad said. "You have to be honest to yourself about who and what you are."

"Be honest about the fact I might eat my friends someday. I get it."

The looks on their faces, though, told me there was more.

"Okay, Dad. I accept the mind lock. But we really have to talk about what you are not allowed to see. After all, I'm not a child anymore." (Take that, Cici!) "And if you acknowledge my maturity, why not tell me everything?"

Cici stared at Dad with a see-I-told-you-so look and he stared back sternly. But eventually, he slowly nodded in what looked like acquiescence. Cici beamed.

"Angie," she said excitedly. "You were probably wondering why I've been around for the past few years. Why I moved back home."

I had wondered about this in the past because Cici was in a long-term relationship with Satchel, a hunky, electricity-channeling realtor from Los Angeles.

"I'm here because of you. Aurora helped me during my change and now it's my turn to help you as much as I can. To initiate you."

Three-hundred-forty-eight year-old Aurora was the next-youngest of my five brothers and sisters. She lived in Sweden, and respectfully declined to embrace the mortal pretense our parents touted.

"Roro was an amazing help to me. The same way Addy was to her."

"So, you're saying we have a tradition in the family? That the next-oldest helps the youngest go through...The Change?"

"Yes," she confirmed. "It's the way our family's done it for a long time."

The thought of Cici helping me through whatever was coming filled me with a sense of peace. Besides my session at Mr. C.'s, it was the only time that day that I felt relaxed. My mouth formed around a potentially skull-cracking yawn before I stuffed a forkful of cold potatoes into it.

"Why would I need your help?" I asked while chewing. "I mean, doesn't The Change just happen on its own?" I chomped on a piece of chicken.

"The shift is not just a physical change, sis, it's total; emotional, mental, even spiritual. It's good to have someone who can be with you."

"For those times when I forget my shoes, find myself levitating uncontrollably, or becoming one with doors," I said in a wry tone.

We all laughed then, loudly and with abandon. Our voices tinkled like the crystal chandelier hanging overhead. But underneath the laughter, there was a sad feeling; we knew we'd never laugh this way again. The "baby" was a baby no more. The family would yet again change. Forever.

The last thing I remember of that night was the way the light glistened on Mom and Cici's teeth, and how it danced in Dad's eyes.

I never made it to my room. In a couple of seconds, I was sleeping like the dead with my head on the dining room table.

8. FIRST SESSION

True to their word, Jules and LaLa came in the morning to pick me up on the way to Sawyer's. When they found out both Mom and Dad were onboard with my career choice, we traded hugs and high fives.

"Are they really letting you drop out before graduation?" Jules asked in an awed tone.

Oops. Had to back-pedal on that one. The answer was yes, but of course I couldn't tell them why. "Nope. Can't have everything, I guess." We climbed into LaLa's old 1995 Saturn.

"Speaking of dropping out of school, " Jules said, "last year, when he was a freshman, Sawyer Creed dropped out of Berklee College of Music to produce full-time."

"Seems to have worked out for him," LaLa whispered later as the three of us looked around his home studio.

As if it were the sole lived-in part of his home, the studio was the only area that was furnished. It took up most of the first floor of his two-level brownstone apartment and featured two large black leather couches, several beanbag chairs, armchairs, fold-up chairs, stools, and various functional tables. A sound booth big enough to hold ten people stood adjacent to a smaller sound booth containing a huge console with a soundboard, Macintosh computers, monitors, and some other cool stuff. Stacks of *Billboard*, *Music Business Journal*, and other music industry mags were sprawled on a low table made from a sheet of Plexiglass balanced on two large concrete blocks.

Sawyer moved around the space like some type of blond tiger, frustrated with not being able to pull the perfect track for us. He was no friendlier than he was the day before, aside from an abrupt hello when we arrived. And, yep, he still frowned. I figured it must be the music that always occupied his head that gave him that perpetual scowl. Did he ever smile? Or even laugh?

He swore under his breath.

"Why don't we just listen to the tracks and pick what we like?" I said to his back.

He aimed his glare in my direction. "That's a lot of tracks."

His bad temper wasn't going to ruin my day. I smiled at him. "Then we should probably get started."

I felt better today than I had in a long time, for a lot of reasons. One: I'd slept for twelve straight hours the night before. Two: telling my family the truth filled me with relief. And three: I was finally going to learn exactly what The Change was. Cici had a presentation called "Bighead's Transformation" planned for the evening. I chuckled at the memory of her enthusiasm when she'd told me about it.

Sawyer raised his head from the sound deck to throw me a nasty look. "Something funny?"

Well, excuse me for breathing. What was his problem? The edges of my vision turned a pre-Shimshana pink.

"Private thought," I said turning my attention to the music videos on the flat screen.

Ironically, none of my thoughts were private anymore now that I was in the mind lock. When I woke up that morning, Cici was floating in the corner of my room, legs folded in lotus position. Her eyes were shut and she looked like she'd been that way for a while. I spotted a glass of juice and some grapes on the nightstand and downed the contents of the glass.

She opened her eyes. "How're you feeling, Bighead?"

"Thirsty." I glanced at the empty glass in my hands. "Guess I'm not Shimshana yet."

"Nope. The Change will take a little time. Could be days or weeks. Definitely on your way, though." She floated to the bed and settled down on the pink comforter. "First order of business. Mind lock."

I sighed, remembering my promise to Dad.

"Don't worry about Dad seeing all your secrets. You won't be locked to him. You'll be locked to me." She smiled broadly.

"Huh?"

"Dad said it was okay when I pointed out it would be the same result whether you were locked to me or him. And in the end, he really didn't want to know exactly how grown up you are."

I breathed a gargantuan sigh of relief. She pointed to my small altar in another corner of the room. On it, below an ancient wooden cross, she'd placed a small blue candle, a small bowl of water, an offering of fresh flowers, and some sort of dried herb. Beside the chalice lay a small ceremonial knife and two miniature goblets.

"Ready?" she asked.

I knelt before the altar and felt the first twinges of apprehension. After all, I'd never had a mind lock before.

She began. "I call upon protection from the Four Directions. Earth." She placed a few of the grapes onto the altar. "Fire." She lit the blue candle. "Water." Dipping her fingers in the bowl, she said "and air" before exhaling and resting her hands on my head. "Mind of my mind, heart of my heart, sisters for eternity. We are bound forever. Now, you say it."

I repeated the words.

"Our minds are one, our hearts are one, where you go I go," she continued. "There is nowhere in this world you go that I cannot be. Do you agree?"

"Yes. Mind, heart, and soul," I said. Before I knew what was happening, the palm of my hand was slit with the knife. "Ouch!" She squeezed a few drops into one of the goblets and drank.

"Now you," she said cutting her wrist just as quickly, letting the blood drip into the other goblet.

I hesitated. It wasn't the first time I would taste blood. Mom had given me some when I was six and too dumb to know any better. I'd been traumatized by that rusty, slippery taste ever since. I took a deep breath, held it, and downed the liquid as fast as I could without being rude.

"Blood to blood, flesh to flesh, your mind is my mind. And so it is."

"And so it is."

We both blew out the candle. The tug of her mind on mine felt comforting.

She glanced at me and raised an eyebrow. "Well daggone it Angel, why didn't you tell me you had to pee!" She hooted as I ran to the bathroom.

# # #

Sawyer's moving goatee-framed lips drew my attention back to the present. I focused my attention on them in order to digest what he was saying.

"There's a hundred and eighty-two tracks here," he said. "I'll play the first few bars of each. Just let me know what you think." His sideways glance seemed to say, "See? I took your advice" as his arm reached over the board to hit "play."

A track started beating out a simple rhythm. As he sipped a bottle of mineral water and watched us intently to gauge our reactions, I wondered if he knew about that old-fashioned production myth—the one that says women are the sounding boards of choice when it comes to creating beats, and if we start dancing it usually means the track has better Top 10 potential.

We listened to the beat with no interest at all.

He hit the delete button, and the next track began. This one was upbeat and bouncy, with a good hip-hop backbone. Julietta started nodding her head, LaLa started chanting a few rap lyrics and I started riffing a little. But after a few seconds, I stopped. Sawyer's eyebrow arched inquiringly and I shook my head "no." "Eh," LaLa declared. He hit delete. We went through quite a few tracks this way, some getting a lukewarm response, some getting no love at all.

After the twenty-sixth track, I turned to the girls. "Edge," I said. "We need it."

Julietta looked dubious. "Nina says to keep it less hip-hop and more pop."

"Should we be trying to sell the record before we even write the damn thing?" LaLa's tone was ironic. "Let's just do what we feel."

"What about track No. 8?" I asked.

They looked at me, trying to recall. I started singing the melody line, note for note, to help them remember.

Sawyer's gaze was sharp. "That's quite a memory you have." Perceptive, I noted, adding that attribute to my mental Sawyer file.

"I take good notes," I lied, gesturing toward my laptop and small notebook. I always kept a notepad or something nearby for times like these so as not to draw attention to my knack for remembering almost every musical arrangement I hear. Changing the subject, I continued with a sense of urgency. "There's a rock guitar with that, something like..." I started singing a counter-melody.

With a deeper frown, Sawyer turned back to the board and pounded a button to start No. 8 again. I sang the melody of the guitar I heard in my head along with the track. Somehow, his frown looked pleased.

"That's tight," Julietta said. LaLa started paging through her lyrics and softly chanted what she found, just loud enough for us to hear her flow, but not enough to distract from the process of putting the different song elements together. Focused on finding just the right sound, Sawyer whip-swiveled his chair around to the keyboard and pounded a number of keys until he located the rock guitar voice.

"That's it," I proclaimed, "that's what I hear."

Nodding his head, he started playing chords in the rock guitar voice, searching for the right combination in the key I sang. Meanwhile, Julietta tweaked a harmonic vocal to counteract mine. On my laptop, I pulled up lyrics I'd jotted down during history class and started singing, while still allowing the track to breathe as we all worked out our contributions.

Suddenly, Sawyer hit a specific chord combination and we cheered simultaneously. "That's it!" I exclaimed. It was exciting to hear him play it the exact way it sounded in my head. His face broke out in a grin as he added the chord to the track and started synching it up to loop and flow along with the beat.

Underneath the excitement of creative synergy, I was disconcerted by his gleaming grin and wondered why the sight of it made my stomach jump. His body swayed slightly as he worked. As his long fingers splayed effortlessly across a wide span of keys, the thick gold ring on the middle finger of his right hand caught the light. His hair wasn't pulled back today. It fell forward in a wavy curtain hiding his face as he bent over the keyboard.

Something, however, was odd about Sawyer: he was excited about the music, too, but his heartbeat didn't accelerate. Mine was beating faster now; so were LaLa's and Jules'. But, come to think of it, his heart had beat at roughly the same rate since I'd met him, despite his mood or level of activity. Maybe he was always calm, even if he only looked excited, or maybe he was in great shape; but either way, it was weird.

I focused back on the music, singing the lyrics over and over again while Julietta and LaLa worked to solidify harmony and rhyme.

It sounded absolutely, positively awesome.

"That works," Sawyer said in an understated tone that made everything feel even more exciting. He jotted down some notes as we high-fived. "I'll dump that on a work CD for you," he added. "Let's move on to the next track."

He hit the play button and track twenty-seven began. "Boring," Julietta said before shooting an apologetic smile at him.

"Not a problem," he said in a friendly tone, "tell it like you see it." He obviously liked straight talk. I put that into my file, too, while noting his more chilled-out demeanor.

The doorbell rang and soon an ultra-skinny guy walked into the studio. He wore baggy, immaculately pressed, dark blue jeans and Timberlands. A gigantic watch hung off his skeletal wrist. Freshly braided cornrows peeked out from under the rim of his pristine baseball cap as he traded fist pounds with Sawyer and tossed his thick, goose-down jacket into a corner.

"Heist is a Quake intern," Sawyer said as an introduction. "He'll take your orders for lunch."

Heist politely flashed a platinum grille. "Hello, ladies. Nice to meet the minds behind 'Get Out of Here.'"

He referred to what was, as far as our fans were concerned, our signature tune. After we'd won the contest, I'd written the lyrics about feeling trapped in a life of pretense, and LaLa had added a blistering rap about rising above hypocrisy. The song lived in an edgy track co-created by the three of us on Julietta's simple keyboard. It was written up in *The Boston Phoenix* as an "underground hit," and was probably responsible for helping to clinch the deal with Quake.

Out of one of the many pockets of his jeans, Heist pulled out a Blackberry. "So, Sawyer already gave me his order, what are y'all in the mood for?"

"Extra spicy Thai soup," Julietta said in her I'm-coming-down-with-a-cold voice.

"Pizza with artichoke and peppers. Salad. And green tea. Please," LaLa requested. Heist looked at me expectantly. I tried to think of something to order, and drew a blank.

"What'd you order?" I asked Sawyer.

He was caught off-guard, as if someone asking him about what he wanted was unusual. "Soul food from Nathan's Hut. Wings, greens, candied yams."

I swallowed down a strong wave of nausea even worse than last night, mindlessly requested pizza, and couldn't even remember the toppings or drink I asked for. Heist jetted out on his mission.

LaLa stretched. "He came right on time. I'm starving," she said before going to search for a bathroom.

"You got any lemon and honey up in here?" Julietta yelled from the kitchen. Sawyer went to assist her.

I assessed my feelings of nausea. I hadn't eaten anything today, and the only thing I'd drunk was Cici's blood.

Is today the day I turn Shimshana?

But Cici told me I had at least a few days. I recalled drinking her blood earlier that morning and waited to see if the memory evoked feelings of hunger. Nope, I concluded after a few moments, I was still as grossed out as before. Maybe I just wasn't hungry.

I wandered over to the boards, fascinated with the complexity of Sawyer's equipment and its many buttons and flashing lights. The large monitors played the waves of track number twenty-seven, and I was mesmerized by the colors and lines that pounded to the rhythm of the beat.

I heard his heartbeat and felt the heat of his body before his voice sounded behind me. "The flashing red button to the left will shut that track down if you press it," he said near my right ear.

I pressed the button. The monitor's dancing waves and colors immediately died. He continued to stand behind me, and the hairs on the back of my neck rose as if a waft of cold air had just entered the room. I smelled freshly showered soap scent mixed with the smell of his skin— mmmm, spicy and sweet—and was reminded of cake batter I'd lick from Mom's bowl when I was little. His lean, muscled arm dusted with light-brown hair reached around my left side to point at a dark button on the board.

"This here's the delete button. You want to send that track to the trash?"

"Yes," I said after a breathless pause, in which I savored the slow drawl of his Georgian accent. I pressed the "delete" button, and a low sound bite of a maniacal clown laugh confirmed the file's deletion. I giggled at his dark sense of humor. But my smile instantly dissolved once I turned around. He was standing so close that I had to lean back slightly with my thighs resting on the edge of the keyboard. His proximity had an overwhelming effect on me.

It was like I was surrounded by an electric circle of Sawyer aura and nothing existed outside of it. I took a deep breath, and his scent entered my nostrils.

And then something weird happened.

The aroma of him—his skin, hair (and other things I couldn't even identify)—traveled down my throat and entered my stomach...where it was met with a loud, undeniable growl.

I *was* hungry. But not for food. I was hungry for Sawyer.

Panic rose as I looked up to meet his eyes. He gazed back steadily, as if examining a strange piece of art. From a distance my mind shrieked; *Sawyer is food!* But I straightened up and moved closer to him. He took a small step back, his eyes never leaving mine. The sound of his heartbeat was the background music banging in my ears as I, in a daze, took another step forward. My fingers itched with the desire to pull through the gold-tinged hair hanging less than an inch from my face. His eyes narrowed and his head cocked to the side. He was exposing his neck...yes, as if he was offering it to me. I inhaled his scent again and my brain switched off.

Led by my watering mouth, I closed the gap between us and placed my lips on his neck.

9. BLOOD, DEATH AND TEARS

My teeth never touched Sawyer's skin.

STOP BREATHING! Cici's voice was deafening and shrill in my head.

I followed the instruction and the spell was broken. What had I done? Scared at how close I came to doing I didn't even know what, I scooted sideways, like a crab, along the edge of the board and out of his proximity.

He looked confused about what just happened. "Angel...?"

I'd run out of air and was in danger of breathing in his scent again. *Go outside. NOW!*

I ran to the front door, stepped out, and sat on the top step. Confused and close to tears, I desperately sucked in the cold winter air.

The good thing about having a sister who can fly is that you never have to wait for her too long. Cici soon bounded up the steps from whatever hidden spot it was she had dropped out of the sky. She reached into her backpack and pulled out a slim thermos. "Drink," she ordered. The smell wafting out of the metal container confirmed it was blood. Before I could even think about it, I drained it quicker than you could say, "Type A."

And that was that.

No trumpet fanfare. No divine choir singing from parted cumulus clouds or anything else I'd fantasized would accompany such a momentous occasion. Nonetheless, I was now a bonafide blood drinker.

I broke out in a cold sweat. "More," I said. Forehead wrinkled with concern, she drew out another thermos. And another. On the fourth, Julietta popped her head out the door.

"Oh, hi, Cici."

My sister, ever the socialite, got up to give her a huge hug while I downed the rest of the blood. "How's it going?" Cici asked after throwing a quick glance at me.

"We're up to track number twenty-eight." Jules rubbed her upper arms against the winter chill.

You still hungry?

My stomach's not growling anymore.

Stay as far away from him as you can. Keep sipping every ten or fifteen minutes. I'll come get you when you're done.

"Then I won't keep you guys," Cici said out loud. She brought out two more thermoses and offered them to me. Julietta grabbed one.

"Wouldn't recommend it, sweetie," Cici said to Julietta. "You sound a little hoarse, and this might make whatever you're starting to come down with worse."

Yeah, you're right," Jules said, unaware of Cici's power of suggestion. Cici calmly took the thermos out of Jules' hands and handed it to me. "I'll pick you up later, sis." She punched my arm and headed into the flow of mortal life known as Commonwealth Avenue.

I felt right again. Jules and I went back inside, where a frowning Sawyer had already fired up the next track. The undecipherable look on his face told me that he, too, had put the incident on the back burner. For now.

The work pace quickened as we continued to delete tracks that didn't work and modify those with potential. Some tracks had samples taken from a number of lesser-known operas, and there were tracks with rock riffs, country, and even blues samples. The diversity of his choices made me feel guilty for having dissed his skills.

Soon we had six hot tracks to build our vocals on, and by the time Heist returned, we'd gone through an additional ten and identified two more to work on. Sipping blood from the thermos, I looked with disinterest at the food Heist brought. Sawyer retreated with his lunch somewhere upstairs, while LaLa tore into her pizza and Julietta slurped down her soup. I was completely grossed out.

"Want?" LaLa asked while gesturing toward my pizza.

"Go for it." I said.

"Your tongue's so red. Thanks."

She tore into a slice. Cheese pulled in long strings from her mouth. I looked away in private disgust and sipped more.

After lunch, we threw ourselves back into picking out tracks from the remaining files and settled into a groove of listening, contributing, amending, and critiquing. Sawyer had become slightly more talkative, but not by much. I chose the chair farthest away from him and he chuckled.

"Something funny?" I threw a dark glare at him.

"Touché," he quipped, turning his attention back to the board.

As we worked, Heist would pop in with packages, which he'd place quietly on one of the couches before heading out again. "Efficient," LaLa remarked while watching him take the stairs three at a time.

She liked him. Jules' rounded eyes met mine in mutual surprise. This sort of thing, LaLa into a guy, didn't happen that often. She was a rebel who didn't care what she wore, except for her extensive collection of top-of-the-line baseball caps. She always put music first, always had rap lyrics and razor-edged poetry bubbling at the edge of her brain or on the tip of her tongue. Because of her strong non-girlie-girl personality, most dudes were oblivious to her, and she to them. But Heist, with his easy-going confidence, was one of the rare ones who caught her eye.

We were waiting for Sawyer, who'd stopped to calibrate some doohickey on the back of his keyboard where a mass of wires lived. He finally finished, sat on his stool, and started banging out Beethoven's "Prometheus Overture" so rapidly the maniacal pace seemed to propel me to another place.

Suddenly, I was downtown and surrounded by buildings. I recognized the office building where Mom worked, B.O.R. International. But I wasn't actually there. My body was still in the studio, and what I saw felt like it was viewed through some sort of tunnel.

It hit me then. I was seeing what Cici saw.

So the mind lock was a two-way street. She could see and experience what I was doing, and now I saw what she saw and felt what she felt. The mind lock was responsible for the mellow feelings I'd had all day (with the exception of wanting to eat Sawyer). It was as if I was bathing in an invisible stream of chill. It made sense that Cici, the most chilled-out person I knew, would rub off on me.

But now she was a bunch of nerves, desperately wanting to get close to Mom and tell her something. Mom's office was on the top floor of the building, and I could feel Cici's frustration at having to adhere to the modicum of "normalcy" that dictated she take the slow elevator as opposed to flying up there. By the time she got to the top floor, she was about to jump out of her skin and I was fidgeting in my chair with her anxiety. The receptionist, whose name, as I remembered, started with a Q, greeted her before speaking into the intercom. Cici moved forward into the office as soon as we heard Mom's terse, "Let her in."

Mom wasn't alone. A man with black eyes turned to Cici and I fought back a shiver as she locked her mind down. She didn't want to know what was in this guy's head either.

"Charleston, it was a pleasure seeing you again," Mom lied. "Quenee will see you out."

Charleston rose and left with the receptionist. The door closed behind them, and Cici turned to Mom. "She's drinking blood."

That was it? That was what she was so anxious to tell Mom? Why not just call or send an email? What was the big deal? Cici collapsed into a chair, her mind on the auto-lock she used around family. Mom sighed heavily and for a frightening second the color drained from her face. I'd never seen her look so tired, and her uncharacteristic gesture, putting her head in her hands, made me want to cry.

"What's happening to her, Mom? She's not supposed to drink blood before she transforms. I don't understand."

Mom straightened up. "Sweetheart, there are no hard and fast rules for The Change. Especially for Angel. She is different."

Different?

"How?"

"We are not sure yet."

Perplexed, I digested this information. Mom was pretty old, and her vast range of experience usually supplied an answer to any question. Why not this one?

"What do we know so far?" Cici asked.

"We know there is a hidden part inside her consciousness. It is a place your father cannot access, even with her permission. He discovered it last night when he touched her temple. That place seems to have an awareness of its own, but she herself is unaware of it. I believe this unconscious element will make itself clear after The Change."

"And the drinking of blood while mortal is a part of this mystery?" Cici asked. "Have you ever seen someone do this before?"

"Yes. Your brother Tunde."

Brother? I went numb with astonishment. I never knew anything about a brother named Tunde.

"He drank blood before his change, and then went on a killing rampage."

My brain started swimming.

"Did he have this hidden place, too? Like Angel?"

"I do not know. But we do know there was something in Tunde's makeup that contributed to his eventual personality. At the time, we did not recognize the specific traits, but we see some of the same traits in Angel."

Hands on my shoulders pulled me out of Cici's head.

"Angel, you okay?" Julietta looked worried.

"Yeah," I gulped. "I was just somewhere else."
Sawyer's hooded eyes regarded me thoughtfully.

I tried to shake the yucky feeling of dread, but between being in Cici's head and recalling Mom's words, I failed. I reached for a thermos and decided to lose myself in the music.

LaLa had a great verse for track No. 97, and to strengthen the rhythm of her flow, Sawyer suggested stepping into the sound booth to record her idea. Julietta joined as a human beatbox, and Sawyer went in with a jimbe drum to beat out the rhythm of the track. Someone had to sit at the board, so I volunteered.

It was also a good way to stay away from all of them.

"Apple Pro Logic DAW," Heist said as he plunked himself down beside me. "Can't wait 'til I get my own." He pointed to the monitors. "Down there, he's got the turntable set up. This board can mix analog as well as digital, so he can throw in all that obscure stuff you heard. He gets a lot off vinyl." He pointed to a collection of actual vinyl albums in a cabinet. I nodded in awe and took a long swig from the thermos.

Sawyer's movements in the booth caught my eye. He was giving me the signal. I hit the "record" button and the console lit up like a bunch of crazy fireflies. The track started and Heist lowered the levels slightly. LaLa started spitting her rap and Heist's head started nodding in time. She'd found a true fan in him, and maybe something more, seeing the way he watched her through the window.

They finished the eight bars. Over the intercom, Sawyer suggested a second take; and Julietta agreed, saying she heard a counter-melody in her head. With a nod, he gave the signal once more. I pressed the button again. As the track began, I heard yet another melody in harmony with Julietta's. Excited, I sang the melody line before belting out a rift that complimented LaLa's peppery delivery. My eyes were closed as I felt the track's hypnotic rhythm mix with LaLa's flow and the melody I was singing. I opened my eyes and my peripheral vision took in Heist, who seemed like he was rocking to the music. It wasn't until he started to fall when I realized there was something wrong.

Heist was convulsing.

Maybe an ingrained respect for the soundboard caused him to fall not forward, but to the side to avoid interrupting the recording process as he hit the floor, where he gasped for breath. I pounded the intercom button. "Sawyer! It's Heist!"

Sawyer raced out of the booth and ran to Heist's jacket, where he extracted an inhaler. He applied the medication, but there was no response. I began pumping Heist's chest and Sawyer breathed into his mouth. CPR. One one-thousand, two one-thousand, repeat. Still, I heard no heartbeat from Heist. LaLa frantically screamed into the phone with 911. But it was too late. Heist, the intern who showed so much promise, was gone.

Sawyer stubbornly kept breathing into him. Stunned, I stopped pumping and eventually Sawyer, struck with the futility of our efforts, stopped too.

Julietta, crying, turned to LaLa and reached for her hands, which had turned into bloody fists from beating the floor. I saw the blood flowing from her hands, but it left me cold. This scene felt too much like when Mr. C. passed out over the keys. And then there was what Mom said. There was something about me, and it was causing people to get hurt. Or drop dead.

The panic started deep in the pit of my stomach. I scooted on my bottom along the floor into the nearest corner, where I cowered in horror. *I'm almost there*, I heard Cici's voice. *I'm calling Dad. Stay calm!*

Her command came too late as a wave of panic took control and lifted me off the floor. To keep from floating into the air, I scuttled under the soundboard, where I fit perfectly in the small space between the bottom of the board and the cabinet with the hard drives. My head was pressing painfully into the board. Crying and terrified, I gripped the heavy feet of the console to keep my skull from being crushed.

Sawyer, his eyes glazed, looked up from where Heist's body lay and saw the state I was in. "Angel, you did all you could do." His voice broke as he reached for my hand.

The doorbell rang. I heard Julietta say, "Dr. Brown...?"

Dad swept in and took in the situation with eyes that missed nothing. "I was only a few blocks away and on my way to the hospital when I heard the EMS call," he explained. He knew immediately Heist was dead, but had to go through the mortal motions of making sure. As he did, his lips moved quickly, as if he was chanting a spell under his breath.

I felt calmer. Soon, I came back down to the ground, and with the pressure around my head and shoulders gone, I could breathe properly again. I sucked in a large amount of air.

Dad made a note in his book and put away his stethoscope. "He's gone," he announced before administering to LaLa's bloody hands. "I'm sorry you kids had to go through this." EMS arrived through the open door. Dad gestured toward Heist's body, shook his head with meaning, and gave the time of death. "They're in shock," he added and pointed to the rest of us. The second attendant started with me, as if I looked like the one in need of the most help.

When Cici arrived, she went to everyone in turn, helping to distribute water, blankets, and words of encouragement. My body was numb and felt strangely distant. I watched Cici, thinking she should have studied medicine instead of architecture. She caught my eye and continued talking to LaLa as she broadcast her thoughts to me. *Dad cast a spell to calm you down. You were freaking out, and now you won't feel much of anything until we get you out of here.*

I was too exhausted to even nod in acknowledgement. After a little while, she finally came to me. "I'm taking her home," she said. They all stared at me.

You look catatonic, Cici conveyed in order to explain the concerned looks on their faces. They regarded me as if I was the second casualty.

And I guess I was.

Because in some way I couldn't explain, I knew that if Heist hadn't sat down next to me he'd still be alive. I failed to stifle a low moan.

Dad directed Cici to take me home and straight to bed, and to keep me warm along the way. *Let them think Angel is in shock,* I heard his telepathic instruction clearly. *She is changing and this will be the cover for why they will not see her for a while. I will be home soon, after I accompany the body back to the morgue and do the necessary paperwork.*

I walked like a zombie. Cici, fighting the urge to pick me up, bundled me in my coat, gathered my things and assisted me. I hated what I was becoming and wanted to die, too.

"You'll get your wish soon, sis," Cici whispered into my ear as we slowly moved down the steps, down the block and into the cover of night. "Tonight you go home to die."

And with that, she rocketed off the pavement with me curled up and weeping in her arms.

10. DEATH OF ME

The sound of screaming woke me up. I was confused, until the violent-colored sound waves pouring from my mouth clued me in.

I was the one screaming.

It felt like my skin was being torn apart inch by square inch and stitched back together. My eyes felt like bubbling eggs in a frying pan. The angle from which Cici looked down on me told me I was lying on my back, probably in my bed. Could I move? I wasn't sure; my body felt like a lump. No arms or legs, just throb. *Cici… Help me!*

It's The Change, Angel. The Shimshana rite of passage. She turned away. "This is my fault. I stupidly thought I had enough time to take you through everything, as if it were a class. I was a silly fool." She turned back to me, and her eyes glowed a faint red. "Crash course. Your body's becoming immortal. It's literally changing as I speak. It's changing as you scream. You may feel as if your skin's being ripped apart. That's because it is. The molecules and the cells are evolving into a different substance. This is the death of you. And the birth of you."

"How long?" I panted.

"Three days."

Seriously?

Suddenly it was clear why The Change had been such a mysterious topic. If I'd known it would hurt this much, I'd have jumped into the Charles River.

"This is how we come to be. Shimshana. We're not made, we can only be born. You'll emerge from the fire like a phoenix. Still hear me, Angel?"

Yes! I thought through the murky agony. My mouth was incapable of making sane sounds.

"There are many blood drinkers. Some are invincible; others are as weak as the smallest insect crawling along a gravestone. And then there are many in between. We're the prototype."

She said all of this matter-of-factly while placing a wet towel on my forehead. It steamed on contact with my skin.

"Yes, you're burning up, but that's normal. Your body temperature's rising and will stay much higher than your old mortal temperature. Now you, too, can turn rooms red, just like Mom."

I tried to laugh, but my teeth, gums, and lips hurt too much. Just then there was a tearing that sounded like something emerging from the area of my stomach.

"Your new digestive tract. It is changing into one that processes blood effectively." This was Dad's voice, and I opened my eyes to see that it was now night. I must have fallen asleep, or passed out.

Kill me now was my only thought.

"You will get the death you wish for." Now it was Mom's voice. "You will die and be reborn to the heat of the sun. It is our natural state to walk in the sun and absorb its rays." Her voice was a soothing drone, as if her intention was to lull me back to sleep. "We are not like vampires, who must hide from the very thing that keeps our planet alive. We *are* alive."

"It hurts, Mommy," was all I could say.

"Leave the pain, Angel." She kissed my forehead. "Separate from it. I know you can do it."

I imagined myself floating over my own body and the pain went away. Ahhh, that felt much better. I looked down at the part of me that was still lying on the bed. I was completely encased in a gauzy, threadlike substance. A cocoon. It shrouded every inch of my body except my eyes, nostrils, and ear openings, which Mom worked to clear.

Again, I wondered how all this Change stuff would affect my life. For the millionth time, I wondered if I'd still be able to sing. What if The Change altered my voice? The agony of this thought, of never being able to sing again, was just as intense as the physical pain, but I couldn't escape it. The mental pain made me cry out with an out-of-body scream that seemed to rip open a hole in the space around me and cause images to rapidly stream through my mind.

There were images of myself, my family, my girls. I even saw Sawyer. There were other faces that only felt familiar, as if I would know them someday. I saw myself singing on a stage in front of masses of people, more people than I ever dreamed would possibly be interested in me. I saw record charts, and sales figures with numbers that made me want to gasp. Was I seeing my future? I knew with my whole being that I was born to sing, and no one or no state of being could take that truth away from me. To not sing would be impossible because my existence depended on it.

As if in response to this revelation, I saw more images; bleak, desolate, and grim. I was angry and alone in a barren landscape. My eyes were solid red, my skin glowed red, and the air around me was dark like a black halo. There were others with me, but despite their clamoring presence, I felt more alone than I even thought was possible.

Bodies covered the landscape as far as the eye could see; bodies of mortals, immortals, and beings I could not identify. I'd somehow killed these beings and a feeling of power rose within me like a dark thirst. I wanted more death, more destruction, and knew without a shadow of a doubt I could bring it. I could make mortals and immortals dance to a different song: the melody of anarchy and the beat of chaos. Was I seeing my life as it could be if I didn't follow the path that I knew with all my heart was meant for me?

I felt a sense of urgency, like if I waited too long I'd lose the ability to make a choice and the darkness would swallow me up. This was more than a vision. It was a decision. *No!* I shouted to the barren landscape and the presences I felt in it. *There is nothing for me here!*

I began to sing. I don't know what song it was, but as I did, the first vision's light continued to grow stronger until it was brilliant and white. And then there were lights as bright as suns... No wait those weren't suns they were...people? An incredible roar...a choir... so many voices singing in a key I'd never heard before. A musical outburst so lovely my soul trembled. Sounds exploded into cascading stars, and all I could do was continue to sing and become one with the beautiful choir. And then the cacophony of glory was in my head, louder, and brighter until I felt like I was being consumed by it.

Underneath it all, a diminutive voice shouted. I stopped singing to listen.

"Can't control it," the voice cried. "It's too strong!" It sounded like Dad.

"Call her back," another voice said. Mom? Were they talking about me? They sounded so far away.

"Angel, come home!" Dad shouted. He was speaking Aramaic, and his voice grew louder by degrees until it was a roar within a roar. "Libero!" he commanded, compelling me to return.

Fighting the pull of the choir, I pushed myself toward his voice. *Dad!*

"Angel! I'm here. We're here."

I followed the sound of his voice until I fell back into my body, back into the pain. I opened my eyes, unsure of what I would see. Mom, Dad, and Cici were all there, all looking at me as if they were looking *for* me. "I'm here," I moaned.

Mom hugged me fiercely, despite my cries of pain. There were tears in her eyes.

"Mom, she's okay," Cici said.

But I didn't feel okay. My eyes were still open, but my family, along with everything else in room, faded into darkness. And then there was no more pain.

"She's dying," I heard Cici say. And then there was nothing at all.

11. ARMY OF ME

I woke up again, feeling fully conscious for the very first time in my life. Every memory I had flashed before my eyes as if I were some breathing camcorder on sixteen-year rewind. I saw everything I'd previously forgotten. The light hitting my eyes when I came out of Mom's body and the immenseness of Dad's face as he looked down on me. I felt Mom's hot hands as she held me close and heard the sound of their laughter. I remembered being held by Cici for the first time and falling asleep in her arms.

I remembered every lame day at school, every conversation I'd had, every gig, and every face in any audience I performed for. But despite the detail, all the memories seemed hazy because up until this moment, I'd been no more than a walking, talking, eating fetus, and my growing body had been a chrysalis. Now, I was really alive and the difference was amazing. Every nerve ending tingled with its own awareness. The pain had been worth it.

My senses were magnified by a million. With just the tiniest effort, I heard every human heartbeat on our block. I wasn't sure how far out the range went, but it sounded like a little more than two hundred hearts. Then there were the heartbeats and movements of the animal life teeming around me. The insects crawling around in the walls were especially loud and annoying. I wanted to dig my fingers into the plaster and remove them one by one to bring the continual slithering sounds to an end. Instead, I tuned out the noise and focused on my new, sharper eyesight. "She's alive!" Cici's excited tones traveled up the stairs. Wow, was her voice always so utterly perfect? Its rays danced before my eyes until I couldn't distinguish between sound and sight. They were now one and the same, for as surely as notes had formed before my mortal eyes, now every sound did, too.

I breathed deeply and it was like sight, taste, sound, and texture were all rolled into one mega-sense. Everything I ever needed to know about anything was contained in all the scents within my range, and the impact of this sensory overload knocked me back on the mattress. I inhaled again.

Oh.

My.

God.

Hunger rocketed me off the bed. Before I even knew I was standing up, I was downstairs in the kitchen, foraging through Mom and Cici's blood supply.

I was ravenous.

I downed an entire pitcher labeled *"MIRANDA"* and I saw her in my mind; short, spiked, dyed-red hair and green eyes with a slight tilt at the corners, like a cat. The scent of her drew me to the foyer and pulled my feet toward the door. The sweet smell of her blood and her taste was so maddening, I laughed wildly and vowed to track her down if it was the last thing I ever did.

"Stop!" Cici barred me from going out the door.

"Whatever!" I started moving forward again.

No, her mind commanded. *Stay where you are. You will not go further.*

"Watch me," I snarled.

Cici floated up and over to the mirror, and her movement forced my eyes to catch a glimpse of myself. What I saw stopped me in my tracks. My hair, fanning around me, was twice as long and reached past my waist. My eyes were darting from side to side, and the pupils were surrounded by a large amount of white. But most frightening was the color of my skin. I was no longer brown. I was bright red.

But none of that even mattered. I still wanted Miranda. I lurched for the door again. My hand and arm passed through Cici's body as she tried to block me. And then I couldn't move. I tried, but the effort was overwhelming. I couldn't even turn my head back or forth, or open my mouth to scream.

"I am sorry darling," Dad said as he walked into my line of vision. "We cannot allow you to go outside in the neighborhood in this condition." He moved his fingers in a one-hundred-eighty degree arch, and as he did I felt my body follow my feet in the same arch, turning around and away from the door.

"She needs to hunt, Dad."

"Then she will hunt," Mom said from the hallway entrance.

Despite my hunger craze, I could see how beautiful my family was. My mortal eyes had been unable to see the golden aura surrounding and emanating from each one. When I looked back in the mirror, I saw that I had a pretty aura, too. My mouth hung open in awe. Then Mom touched

Dad, who clamped his hand down on my right shoulder, and grasped Cici's hand, and suddenly we were surrounded by super-speedy golden light. Lasting a few seconds, it felt like standing on the edge of a freeway and feeling the rush of air from cars zipping by. Then everything was back to normal and we were standing in the woods.

"Congratulations, dear," Mom said. "That was your first space/time collapse." I looked around. The sun shone brightly somewhere, but not here. We were deep in a forest. "We're in Maine," she informed me from where she stood next to a humongous tree. "What do you hear, Angel?"

I could hear the thin keening of the sunlight hitting the massive dome of treetops. The ever-present sounds of millions of insects, which I quickly tuned out. Small, slow heartbeats of tiny animals, and the soft rustling of countless bird wings. A mellow wind fluttered the leaves. Gentle sounds in lavender tones rippled softly like pond waves before my eyes.

"Now, what don't you hear, Angel?"

Human heartbeats. Besides my family's, there were no more for what could have been miles. We were all alone out here.

That's right, sis. We don't hunt people.

"Take a deep breath," Mom urged. "Hold it in."

A delicious aroma assaulted me, and my body instantly tensed like a sprinter at the start line. I turned slightly to see Cici by my side. She was crouched, and her eyes glowed red. Suddenly, her body went rigid. "Listen," she whispered. I heard it, too. Three massive heartbeats, slow and plodding. And they were miles away.

"Go!" Mom said softly, and I took off through the woods. Trees flashed past me in a blur so fast, my feet felt like a part of the ground. Heat rose from the plants, the ground, the very air. It entered through my skin and energized me. The sun hit my face through a clearing in the trees and I stared directly into it. With that, a burst of energy jetted me forward even faster. I felt incredible hunger, wind in my hair, dirt between my toes, and sun energy flowing in waves beneath my skin.

I yelled to Cici, who raced through the treetops above me. "Do we feed off of the sun, too?"

"It makes us strong. But it's the blood that feeds us."

We stopped at the opening of a cave where she touched down and drew in a deep breath. "Bears," she said. "Hibernating. That's why the heartbeats are so slow." She started to enter, but instead of following, I froze. What was I doing? I didn't know how to kill a bear. What technique should I use? Anxiety took hold and my feet left the ground. Obviously, immortality couldn't guarantee peace of mind.

Relax. Observe. She led me, floating through the air, into the cave.

It was easy to see in the inky darkness that before would have blinded my mortal eyes. Like a deadly Goldilocks, I watched three fully-grown bears sleeping soundly.

Take a deep breath, sis. I took several, and touched down.

Cici shook one of them awake. As she crooned softly, crooked a forefinger, and walked to the other side of the cave, the bear followed like a giant, crazy-looking dog and I could feel the power of her mind pressing on the animal's. *Be silent. Follow me.* She patted the bear gently, almost apologetically, before sinking her teeth into its neck. *Do not resist.* It didn't even put up a fight.

Well, that was pretty impressive, but I couldn't do that.

You'll develop your own style. Follow your instincts.

I found myself at the second bear's side. It woke up and glared at me. I didn't know what else to do, so I punched it in the snout. "Oh! Sorry!" I bumbled, stunned by my actions. I felt out of control, driven by the basest of instincts. My stomach growled loudly. Suddenly, my teeth were in the bear's neck, my hair mingling with its fur in a big hairy mass. He put up a fight, but I easily pinned him to the ground with my body. While squeezing a fold of the bear's flesh into a mound between my teeth, I felt my shimshana extend for the very first time.

Shimshana is what we are, but it's also the proboscis we all have that allows us to feed. It stretched out from the center of my stomach, and I groaned in ecstasy as it unraveled its way upward, caressing the walls of my throat before inserting itself into the mound of bear flesh in my mouth. The muscles in my stomach area contracted as the thick warmth made its way down before hitting my stomach with a sharp wave of pain, as if I was eating for the first time in my life.

I felt something weird then, something inside of me, like a light. It began in the pit of my gut and spread through my entire being.

You're feeling the bear's life essence. This happens whenever we feed. You learn things about, and experience an intimate connection to, the source.

I knew all kinds of stuff about that bear. He'd eaten a lot of acorns before entering this cave a few months ago. He'd mated with a couple of female bears around that time, too. He had affection for the other bears in the cave, although they weren't siblings. I felt such epic love for the bear I wanted to cry. But soon, he lay limp on the cave floor as my shimshana retracted quickly back into my stomach. Amazingly, I felt no guilt, even though as a mortal, I'd freak out if I accidentally stepped on an ant.

While considering this, I was knocked face-first to the ground and claws raked deep into the back of my neck. It was the third bear; awake and mad at what was happening to its buddies. I turned as it swiped again, and this time its paw went right through me as if I weren't there. I opened my mouth and roared at the bear with all the rage I felt from being attacked from behind. The inky red black shades in the cave glowed a brilliant red.

Suddenly, the third bear was lying drained at my feet, too, but I had no memory of how he'd gotten there. Cici was gone. Full enough to float away on a cloud of contentment; I walked out of the cave and into the fresh air. My new body processed the bear blood, which thrummed with a hypnotic rhythm in my veins. My legs gave out as a wave of relaxation swept over me, and with a sigh, I sank onto a comfy blanket of snow. Eventually, my parents found me there.

"Well, you look more awake," Mom said. "You've got your normal coloring back."

Cici flashed through the air toward us, then pulled up to chuck a bag of clothes at me. I caught it in a flash. "Closest store was a few miles away," she explained. "Walmart. Took forever at the check out line. Not your favorite Juicy Couture, but you'll live." Dad and Mom laughed.

My nightgown was ripped and covered in all kinds of blood, fur, dirt and skin. Gross. I touched the back of my neck where the bear had clawed me. It was healed. I ducked behind a giant tree to change before making my way back to the clearing where the others were.

"So, dear," Dad said as I made myself comfortable on the circle of boulders they lounged on, "There are a million questions going through your mind right now. You are probably wondering exactly what is going on, and what it all means."

He was wrong. There was only one question on my mind. "What day is it?"

"Thursday," he answered, puzzled.

"Good, I still have time to get ready for the Garden gig." Eager to get back to work, I stood up.

"Angel." Dad spoke as if I were a two-year-old. "You must understand what happened to you over the past few days. You are fully immortal; there is no more for your body to do. Your abilities are almost set in stone, but over the next year you may develop new ones. This is normal. And you are Shimshana. What this means is you must subsist on blood. You will never need to eat mortal food again, although if you want to you can."

"Why would I want to do that?" The thought of mortal food now made me want to hurl.

"We're natural-born immortals," he explained, "and as such, our bodies adapt with time. But change for us is quite different than it is for mortals. Our bodies adapt to the circumstances around us. If not, we would never be able to move with the times. Since our bodies cannot die easily, we cannot allow our other senses to atrophy."

"You said our bodies can't die easily. Has anyone ever died?"

"Yes," said Mom, "my first husband was destroyed. By your brother Tunde."

There was that name again: Tunde. My head started reeling, and I nearly fell head first off the boulder. Dad caught me as I swayed. Cici pushed her calm, and I allowed it to wash over me.

"It was a long time ago," Mom continued. "Tunde was once one of the most loving of souls. But when he started to mature, another side came out. His Mahá was... eventful. Many came away knowing that Tunde was trouble, and our family was devastated at the change in him. He had developed a taste for killing. His powers were immense. He became obsessed with destroying every immortal he could. One day, he decided he was going to kill me."

The blood flooding my mouth told me I'd bitten my tongue.

"I was in the midst of my sleep," Mom continued, "and, so I am told, he trespassed on my resting place. My husband at the time, Levi, caught Tunde in the act. There was a battle between them. I woke up to find Levi in ashes."

I'd always wondered what happened to Mom's first husband. "How did he die?"

Mom took a deep breath. "Tunde was walking fire. In an instant, he could incinerate the most powerful immortal. I stopped Tunde before he could do the same to me."

Dad tenderly took Mom's hand and, in that moment, I was glad that she had someone to travel that long hard road with. "Tunde made some bad choices," Dad said. "It is very important at this point in your existence, Angel, that you decide what kind of life you will lead. Will it be for the good of others? Or will it be something else? After The Change, there is a period of time called the moral window. It is open for about a mortal year, the same amount of time it takes for your powers to fully solidify. During this time, we are faced with tremendous temptation to make bad choices. It is very important to be aware of this and make your decision as soon as possible."

I thought about what he was saying and noticed the way everyone's attention was on me. It was almost as if Cici was holding her breath mentally.

Why was there a question as to what side I would choose? Did it bother me that they had to ask, or did it bother me that I had to think about it?

Dad was still talking. "Your premature blood drinking may have been triggered by your strong connections with your colleagues. If so, your bloodlust might go into overdrive and make your chosen career impossible. You might even kill your entire audience because you feel a connection to them. You have to decide if performing is what you want to do."

Stunned, I sat in silence and contemplated what he said.

"Angel," Mom said gently, "perhaps you should forget the singing career."

I felt it before I saw it. Red. It covered the trees, the ground, the sky, my family. The sun boiled red and every living thing for miles became one big heartbeat that pounded in my skull. It felt like fire raced in my veins. Recalling the horrible vision of a life without music, I opened my mouth and screamed. Angry red sound buckled trees and cracked boulders around us. Birds fell from the sky and snow melted in all directions.

Cici sat still, eyes wide with terror as Mom and Dad looked at each other in the same wide-eyed alarm. A protective field glowed around them; Dad was shielding my own family from me. My heart felt like it was breaking. It occurred to me that I'd killed the second bear with the sound of my voice, and now my voice was destroying everything within earshot. I shut my mouth immediately and only opened it again when I regained some control.

My voice, the only thing I had, was now a weapon. "I'm damned if I do and damned if I don't. What you just saw is nothing compared to what I could do. I saw it. Saw what my life would be if I didn't sing." Feeling hysterical, I looked to Mom. "Death and destruction all around me. I have to sing. I have to sing in order to be good. I want to be good!"

But how could I sing if my voice was a force of destruction? Devastation. I was broken. Blood red tears dropped on the stonewashed Walmart jeans. Mom emerged from the protective field and held me close. We sat in those woods for I don't know how long, and the sound of my weeping filled the spaces between the patches of green moss my outburst had uncovered when the snow melted. Mom stroked my hair while Dad paced back and forth. Cici floated inches above the rocks.

"We can keep the mind lock in place for the next mortal year, until she's completely matured," Cici said.

"We will be in damage control the entire time," Dad replied. "We cannot have more incidents like the boy in the studio."

I wailed at the image of Heist on the floor. "Shhh, no tears, sweetheart," Mom said. "We will work this out."

"Angel," Dad said. "What other abilities do you have? Show us here and now.

Remembering the bear's claws, I said, "Throw something at me. Anything."

Cici tossed one of the dead bushes. It went right through me.

"There is one other thing, but I don't have a mirror." I explained Reflection.

"You're telling me Reflection took on a life of her own?" Cici exclaimed. She was the only one who knew about my "alternate personality."

Mom's face was stern. "Why did you girls not tell us about this before?"

"I don't know," I answered. "It just seemed silly."

Mom and Dad were silent for a moment before Dad turned to me again.

"Angel, you are vulnerable now, but only in that you, like all newborns, may not be aware of the limits of your powers or adept at using them. We get stronger and more in control with time. Even so, it looks like you have a good grip on some of these abilities. The one that is out of control is the most lethal. Your voice."

"Mr. C.," I said. "I think he can help me...not kill anybody with my voice." I told them about the incident in the rehearsal studio and my suspicions about his not being your average mortal. Mom was interested in the latter, and how it might link to why Mr. C. survived when the younger and stronger Heist didn't.

"That is a possibility," she said. "Unless he gets too curious."

"He has been 'curious' about us for years," Dad replied, shifting a glance toward Mom. "Once I heard him think that you were exceptionally beautiful, although he had never actually seen you eat."

"He does have an interesting molecular structure," Mom said.

"The few thoughts I have gotten from him show him to be open-minded and vested in Angel's well being," Dad continued. "I will listen to his thoughts in more detail to ensure he is worthy of our efforts."

"If he can be of use to us without exposing our family," Mom added, "and we can impress upon him the importance of Angel learning to control her instrument, you might have a singing career, dear."

Joy and hope blossomed in my chest. Preparing for the Garden gig now seemed like my only reason for living.

Dad stood up and stretched his legs. "I am hungry," he said. "Everyone else has eaten. And I have lost my food buddy." He patted my knees sadly.

Mom stroked his beard. "I can have your dinner ready in no time," she said.

Dad looked at her lovingly for a long second before saying, "You have been going non-stop for the past three days. You deserve a break."

"I saw a mom-and-pop restaurant," Cici offered.

Dad regarded me for a moment. "It might be an interesting experiment, since you need to be around people, to see how you do."

"But wait a minute. What if I get hungry again? Wouldn't I just kill everyone in the restaurant?"

"It is a possibility," Mom replied, as if we were discussing the weather. "But we have worked out the damage-control process and we can whisk you away before any harm is done." She held out her hands.

"It's next to a gas station, Mom," Cici said, before we whizzed through the ether to stand beside the dumpster away from the pumps. Dad "unplugged" his invisibility spell, and we casually walked around to the front of the building before heading into the restaurant.

The place was packed. We were told there'd be a fifteen-minute wait. Puzzled, we looked at each other, before it dawned on us. "Oh my goodness," Cici whispered. "It's Thanksgiving." With all the drama over the past few days, we'd totally forgotten. Mom's head was bowed as we were led to our table. I took her hand.

"Mom, you've done an awesome job at making it all 'normal' for me, for us," I said. "Please don't be sad. It's not like you didn't have other things on your mind."

Dad pulled out Mom's chair, gesturing to the waitress. "Believe me," he said," I'll be eating every bit of that turkey you have in the freezer. Now that this one isn't eating anymore, it's just more for me!"

We all laughed and I could tell Mom felt a little better.

"What can I get you to drink?" asked the waitress. I stifled a giggle as I imagined answering truthfully. We all ordered some kind of soda. Dad ordered a large amount of food—turkey, stuffing, cranberry sauce, the works. The waitress was shocked to find out it was all for him.

I spied the vein bulging on the right side of her neck. She had an interesting, spicy smell that had nothing to do with the body butter she'd slathered on her skin. I inhaled appreciatively before catching Mom's warning look. Good thing I'd drained two bears instead of one, I thought, as Cici pushed calm on me and Dad chanted a soothing spell under his breath.

The rest of us put in orders for food we had no intention of eating. The smiling waitress sauntered away; unaware of how close she'd been to death.

12. THE NEST

I woke up the next morning wanting to devour
everything. The desire to drink mortal blood was so strong;
I thought I'd lose my mind. "How am I supposed to
function in the mortal world like this?" I complained to
Mom. "I don't even feel sane."

"You are not sane, dear, you are a newborn. And that
means your need for blood can out-shadow all reason if you
do not feed constantly."

Her forefinger smoothed the tired frown on my
forehead. All through the night I'd heard the constant dirge
of various sounds and wondered how one could rest with
all this never-ending noise. I told her all about it after I'd
downed breakfast.

"Do not worry," she said. "Sleep is a habit you will be free of within five hundred years. After that, you can stay awake for decades if you want to. Then, the only sleep Shimshana require is the Great Sleep that comes upon us every seven hundred years or so. Now get dressed, dear. You and I are going to spend some quality mom-and-daughter time."

Within seconds, I was buckling the huge silver belt on my jeans. Before I could say, "who's for brunch," she touched me and we ended up in a massive, posh lounge. I looked around at all the mortals and immortals going about their lives as we walked through. "What's this place?" I asked.

"This is The Nest," Mom answered while pointing to a neon sign that read—surprise—THE NEST. "It is a restaurant/lounge that is part of the Nutrition & Wellness Network."

People were involved in all kinds of activities: talking, watching TV, playing video games, etc. But what caught my eye the most was the sight of people feeding directly from willing mortals. I'd only seen people like us drink from containers. There was one particular couple, a fanged she-vamp and a guy donor. He moaned real low as she drank from his neck, her long red hair tossed casually over one of his shoulders. She gulped him down as their heartbeats pounded together like two racehorses heading toward a finish line.

"In part," Mom continued, "The Nest serves as an urban alternative to hunting. Now, sweetheart, do not misunderstand me. There is nothing wrong with hunting. It is who we are. But we are also so many other things. Civil. Humane. Courteous. In a nutshell, this is a place where you can feed in a way that honors humanity."

She followed my gaze as I continued to stare at the couple. He was still moaning. "It is rude to stare, honey," she said turning my head to look at her. "No matter what type of blood drinker you are, there is a very pleasurable aspect to feeding directly from the source. For Shimshana, it is even more so. If you take the feelings of connection you experience while drinking a donor from a glass or thermos and multiply that by one hundred, you still could not gauge the level of pleasure you receive."

I could feel my eyes pop out of my head. Eventually, we came to a stop. "This is our family's booth," Mom said. We were at a plush red couch in a private candlelit area. There was a low, round wooden table painted black, with elaborate flower designs. Thick burgundy draperies covered the wall behind us. Classical music emitted from speakers on an iPod dock. We sat down.

"Sweetheart, we need to talk about sex."

I nearly choked on the air. "Mom!"

"Yes, I know we talked about mortal boys years ago, but now that you are an adult there are a few more pieces of the puzzle you need. Angel, newborn appetites are the strongest and since you will be hungry for at least a year, the best thing we can do is provide you with your own donors."

Donors? More than one person to drink in? Gulp. This was better than Christmas.

"But with donors comes responsibility. The pleasure you will get when feeding this way can feel very sexual. For both of you. Your donors will be yours and yours only, simply because it will take all they have to cater to you. You will feel strongly connected to them, and them to you. But having sex with them will be irresponsible on your part."

"I know, Mom." I rolled my eyes. "Because I'm saving myself for that special guy."

"Yes, but that is not all. Our donors benefit physically from the relationship. It lengthens their life spans and takes away many of their common ailments. They also heal a little more quickly than non-donor mortals.

"But the other side of the coin is this: donors are vulnerable to us in almost every way. Physically, mentally, emotionally. If we do not encourage them to have lives outside of us, our donors will choose to exist for us alone, and waste their lives living from feeding to feeding. It is our moral responsibility to take care of them on all levels." She took my hand in hers. "Besides, you will know when the right guy comes to you. All of those special feelings you have will be for him alone. Because when we love, we love fiercely, and with our entirety. And he will be strong enough to handle you. I knew that when I met your father."

"Ewww! Can I eat now?"

She inclined her head slightly. Almost instantly, someone was at our table.

"At your service, Elder," he said, bowing deeply.

Mom gestured to me. "My youngest. She needs two. This will be her first time."

"I have the perfect matches. The first will be a young man. It will be his first time as well." Mom nodded her approval as the "waiter" discreetly vanished behind an elaborate partition.

I sat on the edge of the couch, back ramrod straight, hypnotized by the sounds of feeding. I wiped away beads of blood sweat from my forehead. Mom offered me a tissue from a nearby box. "You will not drain your donors, Angel. To do so will kill them." Her words snapped me out of my trance.

"We prefer to keep our mortals alive," she continued. "We leave them with a certain amount of blood so they will remain healthy. If you take the right amount, they will feel slightly weaker, but will be fine once they replenish their energy in the Rejuvenation Center. You are not allowed to take beyond that amount."

She pointed to a bell. I'd noticed earlier that every table had one. The bell was attached to some device that resembled a timer. "Once this bell rings, you must stop," Mom continued. "That is the rule."

I wondered who or what enforced that rule, and what the consequences for disobedience were.

"How do people become donors?"

"They are almost all referrals. Once their application is approved, they go through a background check, screening process, and physical, emotional, and psychological evaluations. The best ones are chosen and waitlisted. Then they go through training. They are compelled to never reveal to any other mortals any information about this place or their role as donors. Once bitten, it is physically impossible for them to give anything away."

"Wouldn't you and Dad be more...ummm...comfortable...if my first donor was a girl?" I looked back at the couple who were now stroking each other, and entwined on the couch.

"It makes no difference, Angel. You are an adult now. Would you like your first to be a girl instead?" Her face was expressionless in a way that only a two-thousand-year-old mom face could be.

I thought about it for two seconds. "No, Mom. I want a guy."

The waiter returned, followed by a tall, muscular guy. He was a little over six feet, and despite the muscles, he had a lean build. Black hair and kind, almost black, eyes collided with brilliant white teeth. He looked a little nervous, but his smile was dazzling.

"This is Justin," the waiter said. "Let me know if there is anything else you require."

Justin sat down and we faced each other expectantly.

"Since this is your first time, they make it a little more instructional than usual," Mom said. She smiled at Justin, and gently tilted his head to the side to show me a diagram drawn on his neck. "Do not worry kids, the marker is non-toxic. You will place your teeth exactly how this illustrates. There is also an instructional brochure in the small side cabinet there. You will have to figure out the rest on your own." She stood and picked up her purse. "You have all the time in the world." She left us alone.

Justin and I continued to stare at each other long after Mom left. I strained to block out the sounds of mealtime from all around The Nest so I could focus on him, but it seemed to be a losing battle.

"So, you're Angel."

"Yep."

I didn't want to make small talk; I wanted to chow down. But how rude would it be to just pounce on him like...a piece of meat? My nails sliced into the palms of my hands as I struggled to control myself. "Are you nervous?" I asked him.

"Yep."

A couple tattoos peeked through the sheer material of his white silk shirt. My stomach contracted in anticipation. He watched me with a friendly yet guarded stare. Smart, since I was the hunter and he was the prey. He wasn't fooled into thinking otherwise by the Nest's elaborately civilized decor.

"I'm nervous, too," I said. "You're my first."

"I've done the training. I know what the deal is." He looked into my eyes, as if to remind me he was not a piece of meat. "But I couldn't have been prepared for a prettier mistress."

Mistress? A mental image of Elvira Mistress of the Dark popped into my head. It made me even hungrier and I moved toward him until we were close enough to touch. "Let's get started."

"Yes, mistress."

"Enough with the mistress stuff, for crying out loud. Please... Just call me Angel."

"Yes...Angel." He tilted his head to the side to fully expose the diagram.

My teeth rested on the delicate skin. Inhale. Mmmm... I couldn't remember anything from mortal life that smelled so good. After a second I gave up trying to think. My impulse was to just be, and allow the wonderful aromas to flood my senses. He waited with his thumb hovering over the start button on the timer.

Deep inside of me, my shimshana started to extend and unfurl. Just as Mom said, the feeling I experienced, now that I was with a person, was sensual... and also amazing, and tingle-y. Yum.

I bit down carefully as the instructions indicated, holding the mound between my teeth gently, making sure not to break his skin as my shimshana probed and penetrated him. He tensed up slightly before relaxing with a sigh, and I wasted no more time. My intestines contracted and sucked him in stronger with each pull. The taste and the warmth was something I couldn't have been prepared for. I soon felt as if I'd known him for years. There was no sense of time, and I was surprised when the bell rang. With great difficulty, I pulled myself out of his muscled embrace as my shimshana retracted.

Justin sighed as he sprawled all over the couch and I sprawled all over him. I rested my head on his chest and could feel his heart pounding a mile a minute. I enjoyed the feeling of us together; it almost felt as if we shared one body.

"Was it good for you." His tone was joking but his face was serious.

"Better," I answered.

And then I was hungry again. After a long hug and exchange of email addresses, Justin was led away to the Rejuvenation Center.

"Number two now," was all I said to the hovering waiter.

13. GETTING THE KINKS OUT

After The Nest, I was as content as a fat cat next to an empty milk bowl. Mom plopped me back in my bedroom before we heard a knock on the downstairs door. Inhaling, I recognized the scent right away. It was Mr. C., ready to help me get a grip on my now-lethal pipes. Cici ushered him in, and, yet again, I was down the stairs before I even knew I was moving. His face registered a few seconds of shock when he saw what probably looked like me popping out of thin air. Mom had told me I was pretty fast. I felt bad for making him feel uncomfortable.

"Hi, Mr. C."

He quickly recovered his face and eyed me for a drawn-out moment, taking in my appearance and whatever else he managed to see with those enigmatic eyes. "Angel. You've been busy."

I grinned. Mom came in. "Mr. Caulkins."

"Mrs. Brown. Please, call me Sheridan."

"Only if you call me Cleo."

He kissed her hand a little too gallantly. "It would be an honor," he said. There was an air of understanding between them now, thick with unspoken words.

I found myself in the kitchen pouring coffee for him and blood for me. Seriously, I was going to have to find a way to slow down if I was going to look normal in the mortal world. The house came alive with the strains of Tchaikovsky as Mr. C. played on the grand piano in the living room. Tchaikovsky was always one of my favorites, but with my new immortal hearing, it seemed like I'd never heard the music before. Varying shades of green and purples with hints of blue danced before my eyes.

It was so beautiful, I grew confused. I fought the urge to go immediately to the living room to be closer to the music. My hands were frozen in the motion of pouring blood, and a puddle formed on the floor as I stood there in indecision. Falling onto my knees, I licked up every drop, knowing this unladylike display would be so uncool with Mom. Sure enough, as if on cue, she walked in.

She took one look at me with my tongue on the floor, one look at the puddle, and pivoted out of the kitchen muttering something about "God give me strength." I continued my cleanup duties without missing a beat. Cici roared with laughter upstairs.

When the floor was all sparkly clean again, I wiped my mouth with a napkin so as not to give poor Mr. C. another scare. I couldn't imagine what would go through his mind if he saw blood dribbling down my chin.

"So Angel," Mr. C. said as I placed his coffee mug and a ceramic coaster down on the grand. "It would seem as we have some serious work to do, my dear."

From my immortal point of view, the only thing different about him was his smell. It was more intense. The tang of his blood and skin mixed with the less organic odors of cologne and cigarette smoke to create a bouquet of age, decay, and resilience. It was an aroma that spoke of many ups and downs, but not enough to really make a dent in the world. It was the fragrance of mortality, and it drew me in like honey attracts flies.

I stayed as far away from him as I could while sipping out of my thermos. He didn't ask me what I drank. In fact, he didn't ask me anything pertaining to me on a personal level. Didn't he sense that I wasn't the same? He was the first non-donor mortal to have any contact with me since I woke up.

"Mr. C. Do I seem different to you?" I'd never been so bold with him.

"Angel, you look the same." His fingers absently tinkled notes on the grand. "But it's clear to me you're not. And I would dare say anyone who loves you and knows you would see that as plain as day. You just need to decide how much you want people to see. Your parents have been very clear with me. Quite honestly, I still enjoy this life too much to want to know more about exactly how different you are. That being said, let's start in the key of C. You will stop singing the very second I say stop. Understand?" I nodded.

He began to play and I started to tremble. I opened my mouth to sing, but no sound came out. I recalled Heist crumpled on the studio floor, had a flashback of the giant grizzly in the cave, and relived the agony of seeing Mr. C. himself crumple over the keys. I began to cry. "Can't," I whined.

"You can, and you will," he retorted. He looked at me kindly, but stayed firmly planted at the keyboard. No grandfatherly hug. He now stayed away from me the same way I stayed away from him. He knew I was dangerous. The tragic reality of this insight made me cry even more. I stopped when I saw the look of utter shock on Mr. C's face.

It was as white as a sheet. He was looking at my tears. My bloody tears. I bawled even louder.

"I'll never be the same," I wailed. "Nothing will ever be the same. How can I sing?"

He calmly unfolded his handkerchief and handed it to me, at extreme arm's length, from where he sat. I gingerly took the proffered white cloth and wiped my eyes. He blinked several times in disbelief as he looked at the bright red smears on the fabric. I watched him gather himself and his thoughts for a while until he said, "I will teach you, my dear. We will start at the beginning and work our way through. I will make sure you perform at the Garden without hurting the smallest fly on the wall."

"So you know?" I asked.

"I've known for years, Angel. From almost the beginning, I knew your voice has power to heal. You see, I'd been suffering from cancer..."

And he told me about how his terminal cancer cleared up shortly after he started working with me. I felt my mouth fall open. The idea that my voice could help people was fascinating, but it seemed too good to be true. "How do you know I had anything to do with that?"

"Sometimes I know things for certain," Mr. C. said. "There may not be a reason in the rational world that I should believe a thing, but in my heart I know it to be true. For the longest time, I asked myself if I was crazy to think that such a thing can be possible. That the voice of a child could destroy cancer. Even after I witnessed your voice crack and then re-seal my drinking glass, I thought that I'd lost myself in a flight of fancy, that I couldn't possibly be in my right mind. But I couldn't deny the wonderful joy, the upliftment I felt after every one of our sessions. As if my soul was taking wing."

To think I could actually do something good with my voice brought hope to what had seemed to be a doomed situation.

"Then I came to a conclusion," he continued. "It didn't really matter whether it was true or not. Just seeing your face during our sessions, and the delight you experience while singing made it all seem possible. You were born to sing, Angel. We who eat and drink music have to look out for one another, you know."

"But I nearly killed you." I gasped again at the horrible memory.

"You didn't kill me. And that's why I know you will find that balance. It is love. Love compels you to sing, and love will compel you to find that balance. Focus on the love in your heart while you sing."

Finding a balance. What he said made sense, but how could I possibly use him as a guinea pig? "What if I hurt you again?" I asked.

Dad put a spell of protection around Mr. C., and we've assured him that he is safe. He's really quite brave. Now listen to him.

"I never felt like I belonged," Mr. C. was saying, "unless I was playing or listening to the music. These feelings, of not belonging, of being somehow different, caused great anger to fester in me. And I would do things that weren't very...nice. My life could have very well gone down a completely different path altogether. Fortunately for me, I had a teacher who knew the potential I had. And I will tell you now what she told me all those decades ago. She said, 'Focus on the love.' So Angel, I want you to feel your love of the music bubble up in your heart. In your soul. Love for your audience. Love for the very sound of your precious voice."

He gently pressed the first chord in C. I drew in a deep, shaky breath, tried to remain calm, and shaped my mouth to let out the corresponding note. It came out weak. But it was enough to crack granddaddy's iron sculpture. The arm of the beautiful goddess figure broke off with a loud snap.

"Stop," he said. And then silence.

He looked at the sculpture for a long moment. Was he reconsidering all of the stuff he told me just minutes ago? In light of the bloody tears and the cracked sculpture, I wouldn't have blamed him if he'd picked up that briefcase and hightailed it somewhere where it was safe. Part of me wanted to warn him, tell him to run and get away from me as fast as his aged mortal legs would take him. Which wasn't really fast at all, and surely no match for me. I shrank into the corner, feeling like a menace to society, a monster to be shunned. I felt so broken-hearted, I couldn't even cry again.

"What is that sculpture, Angel? It seems very old."

"A family heirloom." My voice sounded lifeless to my own ears. "It's been in our family for longer than I even know."

This was the truth. Although immortals had kept meticulous records of family trees and lineages even before mortals learned how to do it for themselves, I was still unsure exactly how old the piece was.

"Fix it," Mr. C. said. "Use your voice to repair the damage you just did. Don't worry about the way you sound. You've got years of technique to fall back on and if you allow it, it will kick in as soon as you take a breath. Right now, you must visualize the sculpture whole again, and focus on that to the exclusion of all else but love."

He played the chord again. Softly, expectantly.

Love. Visualize the love. What would the love I felt for the music look like? I closed my eyes and concentrated. I knew how the sounds themselves looked, but love? I thought about the love I had for the music, how I felt when performing on stage. I contemplated how I wanted to make every person who listened to my music happy.

Love.

How would it look? What color would it be? I supposed it could look like the goddess sculpture. The soft rounded curves, the generous smile, the graceful, elegant pose that spoke of beauty and peace of mind. I stared at the sculpture and imagined it to be the image of love.

The chord sounded softly again. And again, patiently awaiting my vocal response.

It seemed as if the goddesses' smile was slightly bigger than I'd seen it before. And then for a brief moment, it almost seemed as if the sculpture's eyes came to life. They were loving, and they were looking at me. Before I knew what I was doing, I'd opened my mouth and the sound came out; a shimmery pink note that wafted gracefully around the room. I was singing the word "love."

Mr. C. beamed like a proud daddy. "Yes! That's it. Keep singing love."

He climbed the scale as I continued to follow, tentatively sounding the word, but eventually feeling more confident as we went along. Mr. C. was right. I really could sing without killing. I decided that I would never go back to that dark place where people dropped like flies at the sound of my voice. I determined that, from this point on, my voice could be a tool for healing.

I focused on the goddess sculpture again, this time imagining it complete, with the little arm where it belonged. I purposely directed the sound waves toward the sculpture. As I did, the luminous pink waves flowed into and around the goddess; and soon the arm was back on as if it had never broken off.

"Stop, Angel!" Mr. C. said. "That's it! Remember what you just did. That is the sound of love. Now. Let's try it in the key of D."

14. THE LAW

Later on, in my room, I was exhilarated, exhausted, and relieved to be away from anything having to do with the mortal world. A victory had been won today. I was confident in my abilities to sing without killing, but the session with Mr. C. had worn me out. And there were still so many questions.

Cici dropped a stack of thick binders in front of me. "Million questions? Ask away. Just pick through colors while we chat."

"Colors?"

"For your Mahá, silly. Don't you want it to be hot? Everybody will be there. We have to choose paint, the theme, the music, there's so much to do." She looked me up and down, and sighed. "We really need to do something about your wardrobe. What you wear for Mahá is extremely important."

"What's wrong with what I'm wearing?"

"Everything. The club-kid look is childish. Jeans, hoodies, and the like. Definitely not the type of image you want to portray for Mahá."

I felt the room go hot and saw a haze of red in front of my eyes.

Mom stuck her head in the doorway. "Is someone boiling mad in here?" She carried in more binders and placed them on the bed before plunking down on the floor with one. "You are really going to have to control your temper, sweetheart."

"But Mom, Cici was totally dissing my clothes. She said I dressed like a child." I heard myself whine and stopped. The red haze cleared up.

"Well dear, Cici has your best interests in mind. And there is a lot to be said about the image you project at your Mahá." She opened a binder full of fabric swatches. "You might consider getting fitted for some custom pieces. We have a fantastic tailor, Ms. Thelma, who has been outfitting young ladies for their Mahá since the turn of last century. She is really excellent at what she does." She held up a swatch next to my face. "Midnight blue is one of your colors." She marked it for future reference.

"Why's it so important how I look for Mahá? And why am I picking out colors for paint? Are we really going as far as to re-paint the walls?" Mom and Cici smiled at each other. They were excited about something and although I didn't know what it was, I started to feel it too. "Tell me!" I demanded.

"Start at the beginning, Mom," Cici said as she hit "play" on the iPod dock. London chill-out music started to play in the background. "This may take a while," she continued, "so get comfortable and just keep picking out colors you like. We'll start with the walls and then choose for rugs, window treatments, furniture, dishware..."

I stared at Cici like she had just morphed into a Chihuahua. Surely we weren't redecorating the entire house… for a party?

My stomach growled. Cici flew out of the room and came back in seconds balancing a number of pitchers and glasses. "Drink before you get hungry," she said. "Stay on an even keel."

I took in the aroma of each pitcher and fell into a state of serious indecision. They all smelled so good. Especially Sebastian. I poured a sample, and tasted it. Mmmm…I could clearly visualize his long, dark hair and long eyelashes. I decided to go find him and started edging toward the door.

"Will you really hunt him down, Angel?" Mom asked. "Remember what we talked about. Make the right choice for the life you want to live."

I took a deep breath and, with great difficulty, planted myself firmly on the floor. Picking up the Sebastian pitcher and pouring a goblet-full, I stuck my nose in the glass and inhaled deeply, the way I'd seen the wine connoisseurs do for pinot noir. My throat burned with hunger and my body felt like it was on fire.

Determined to not find myself downstairs again at the front door, I slurped Sebastian down and forced myself to sit still. After ten minutes, they both nodded with approval.

"That's my sis!" Cici bragged.

"I'm very proud of you," Mom said as she gave me a tight squeeze, and arranged a lock of hair that had fallen across my sweaty face.

Just yesterday it seemed impossible that I could ever be around mortals and display any control whatsoever, but today was a new day. Mr. C. had left our house alive. And here I sat drinking Sebastian, feeling totally connected to him, seeing him clearly in my mind down to his height and shoe size. The intimate knowledge of him grew the more I drank. But still I sat. I hadn't raced to the door, and I wasn't beyond reason. Yes, I still wanted to hunt him down, and the desire to absorb his essence into my own was almost maddening. But the feeling was overshadowed by the need to keep him alive so that I could have him again. I saw that for moral (and, okay, I admit it, selfish) reasons, keeping donors alive was better. I took a small sip, savored it, and sat still.

Mom mopped my face with a small towel. "As you know," she said, "The Mahá is an ancient tradition that dates back to Biblical times." She held up another swatch next to my face. This one was a dusty pink silk with thin threads of gold shot throughout.

"Pretty," I said in a half-hearted effort to contribute. Mom nodded in agreement before marking it, too.

"In order to fully understand the Mahá," she continued, "you must first know your own history. Angel, you are the great, great-granddaughter of Star. She was, is, what is popularly referred to as a 'fallen angel.' She and a number of other fallen angels are our ancestors, the primogenitors of our kind."

I'd read about fallen angels, but I'd never dreamed I was reading about my own family. "Fallen angels were evil, I mean *are* evil. Aren't they?" I asked.

"Some make unfortunate choices," Mom said. She ran a finger along a piece of lavender-colored lace before placing it back in the book and moving on to the next page. "Some are trying to atone for their mistakes.

"They came to this existence to help mortal men. Star was one of the Watchers. Their job was to lead the mortals and teach them how to survive. Over time, many Watchers fell in love with mortals and took on human form in order to mate with them. It is said that the Watchers loved mortals so much they rebelled against God. Some took on the form of men; some took on the form of women. Children born of the latter proved to be powerful and immortal. We think it may have something to do with the gestation period associated with being in the body of an angel. Unfortunately, those early immortals frequently murdered each other, mortals, and even themselves. The fallen ones learned the hard way—they had to make things right in order for their children to have better lives.

"Was great, great-grandma Star evil?" I held my breath waiting for an answer.

"No, she is not," Mom said. I let out a sigh of relief. "The ancestors took steps to control their offspring. Eventually, as we began to have families of our own and our numbers increased, there had to be a way to keep track of all the immortals on the planet so that we could know the very answers to the questions you just asked: 'Are they good or are they bad?' The Mahá was created for that very purpose. We are not sure when the first Mahá was, or when it was instituted as law. But we know Star was instrumental in enforcing it.

"The concept of the Mahá is simple. When a child is reborn, the family invites all other immortals to come and see the newest of our kind. They see firsthand what powers and what kind of character the newborn has. Mahá is mandatory for every new immortal, and it is mandatory for every immortal to attend or be formally represented."

"Does every immortal on the face of the earth have a Mahá?" I asked.

"No. Not all are introduced to society this way, but those with no Mahá are considered a threat to every Mahá-introduced immortal. To have Mahá brings one under the protection and acceptance of the Body of Restoration."

"What's that?"

"The Body is a worldwide organization founded by Star and the other fallen ones who sought to atone for their mistakes with humanity. The Body creates and enforces Law for immortal humanity. Without Mahá, one can be eliminated without retaliation or justice. So as you can imagine, most immortals have one."

Cici handed me an old album opened to a black-and-white portrait of her and the rest of our family surrounded by a massive group of people. "My Mahá.1871." In the picture, she looked slightly younger, and her off-the-shoulder gown—a dark, satiny material decorated with dainty flowers—was to die for. She wore mid-length white gloves and a choker around her long, graceful neck. Her elegant hairstyle completed the ensemble.

Most of the family was dressed in similar, if less spectacular clothing, with the men in three-piece suits and top hats. The guests were dressed in formal multi-cultural wear. And then there were others...

I pointed to the short, dark-haired guy in full body armor. "Oh, that's Uncle Garroway," Cici said with a big smile. "He's forever medieval."

"Well," I said, "at least he took off his helmet for the pic."

The group stood on a lawn the size of a football field. Behind them was a cliff with a breathtaking view of the ocean. "We could not have Mahá here in the States, as it would garner too much unwanted attention," Mom explained. "So we bought a plantation in Barbados, one of many that had been abandoned in the wake of slave rebellions. We still own this plot of land and have had many happy memories there." She stroked the picture fondly.

"Your Mahá will be even better," Cici said with excitement. "We have so much more cool stuff now. Digital pictures!"

Mom's eyebrow arched and her mouth formed a stern line. "That," she said, "is proving to be a problem. There is an entire outfit of the Body dedicated to policing the Internet, where a lot of these pictures end up."

"Mahá's the event to end all events," Cici said. "So for your Mahá, not only will we have awesome playlists and live music, we also built a house."

Lately, my mouth had been hanging open a lot, and now was no exception. I'd known that our family was wealthy (how could you not be after centuries of investments?) but all my life we'd lived in a pretty ordinary way. Now it seemed like suddenly we owned land in exotic locales and were building houses for parties.

"It's in L.A., in the Pacific Palisades canyons," Cici continued. "Dad bought the land back during the gold rush. I started overseeing the construction of your house a couple years ago—"

"*My* house? *I* have a house!"

"Yes, Angel, a present for your Mahá, it's so cool, wait till you see it, you're going to flip. And now the work's all done and just waiting for your personal touch. There are even secret rooms. And we've already retained Planned Events."

Planned Events was a company run by immortals who specialized in supernatural events. With PE, all you had to do was plunk down a deposit and it would be held for however long it took for the child to change. They were the best at what they did because their business model could absorb the long waits between making a deposit and actually having the event.

"And wait 'til you see the view, Angel," Cici added with a mischievous grin. "You'll die." We all laughed out loud at the joke. She pointed to a blonde in the Barbados photo. "Her daughter, Grace, had a ridiculous Mahá a couple years ago. They rented out a sheik's palace in Dubai and had some of the biggest rappers perform. There were belly dancers, illuminated yachts, banquets. It lasted for over a week."

"Aren't we supposed to be under the radar?"

"We are," Mom said. "So today's Mahás, like our lives, have a public face and a private face. The performers, and all mortals involved, think they are working at coming-out parties, quinceañeras, bar mitzvahs, cotillions, etc. Mahá law demands that only immortals attend the ceremonies and rituals, and these events are not publicized. For the rituals, there are no cameras, cell phones, or any kind of recording device allowed in."

I gulped down terror. "Rituals? Ceremonies?"

"Don't worry, Angel," Cici reassured. "It's nothing to be nervous about. All very formal and by-the-book."

"The rituals and ceremonies were crafted expressly to introduce the immortals to the rest of the world, and vice-versa," Mom continued. "Remember it is all about getting to know one another. Now, my Mahá was a little frightening."

Both Cici and I stopped thumbing through the binders and gave Mom our undivided attention. She rarely spoke about her childhood.

"My Mahá witnessed interesting visitors. First, there was a five year-old boy. By then, Mahá rules were set in stone and one of them was that only immortals were allowed, thereby leaving out children who hadn't yet matured. But this boy was different. His parents were mortal and had brought him to Egypt to save his life. Immortals in our area, including your grandparents, gave him and his parents asylum by direct order of the Body. I remember being very eager to see this boy who was the object of the wrath of a powerful king, and the recipient of such protection from the Body. He himself was born into very humble surroundings: a manger, they said, alongside animals."

Cici and I gasped. Surely Mom wasn't talking about—

"At first, when he arrived at my Mahá, there was an uproar among a few of the attendees due to his young age.

But among his many companions were several Ancient Ones. That silenced all outcry."

"Ancient Ones?" I asked.

"Our ancestors," Cici whispered. "The Fallen Angels." Mom nodded and continued.

"In the early days, as they tried to bring order to the chaos their offspring caused, the ancestors attended every Mahá and actively enforced the new laws. At first they were seen as parents and then, later on, elders, but over the course of time they became feared as the walking personification of angelic forces on this planet. Even in their fallen state, they were and always will be more powerful than any human immortal. Eventually, the ancestors sent representatives in their stead and only personally attended the Mahás of certain individuals whom they took a special interest in.

"We knew the boy, Jesus of Galilee, was a special guest when they arrived with him and a few of his other companions, who were not of this earth at all. They had all come to see who I was, to get to know me. Things would never be the same for our family after that."

"Why were they there to see you, Mom?" I asked.

"My ability, molecular manipulation, is rare and can be very destructive. If they had determined that I was 'bad,' the Ancient Ones would have destroyed me on the spot. It was the last time I saw Star."

"Where is she now?"

Mom paused and put her binder aside. "No one knows where the Ancient Ones are now. There are stories, myths, that some of them, in their quest to be absolved, were allowed back into the seventh dimension. Others say they exist somewhere between there and this dimension, but no one knows exactly where. We do know they do not live among us anymore, and because of this separation, we now always know when they come."

If we had been sitting on chairs instead of the floor, Cici and I would have been on the edge of our seats.

"When an Ancient One enters this dimension and comes into the vicinity of earthbound immortals, our abilities are weakened and, in many cases, rendered useless until they leave."

I digested this bit of information. "But don't they run the Body of Restoration?"

"They do, but through everyday immortals. The day-to-day global affairs of the Body are run by the descendants who are handpicked by the Council. Council members are well known to the immortal community. They are infallible. They represent the law in a world where there are not many rules. They often act as stand-ins for the Ancients at Mahá."

Cici's heartbeat speeded up, and she had that anxious deer-in-headlights look again.

"You think Ancient Ones will come to my Mahá," I said.

"Oh yes, Angel," Mom said. "They will want to get to know you. And whether you survive your Mahá or not, you, like me, will be filed away in the documents of the Body of Restoration."

Her eyes held mine, and the whites around her glowing red pupils seemed to hover like hot neon. I inhaled with the sudden shock of understanding. "Body of Restoration," I repeated. "B.O.R....You?"

"Yes." Her quiet answer was more frightening than any scream. "As a Council member of the Body, I am The Law. And have been for almost seven-hundred years."

15. BACK TO WORK

Instead of sleeping, I spent the night mentally rewinding my entire life.

Everything I had heard and seen in relation to Mom was infused with new meaning now that I understood what her real job was. All my life I'd thought she was an attorney for a privately held corporation. But that was her public face. Her true job was being a Council member of the Body of Restoration.

Mom was immensely powerful. Council was as close as you could get, in hierarchy, to the Ancient Ones themselves. If the AOs were the Board of Directors, Mom and the other Council members were the Executive Board.

Furthermore, Mom would act as the B.O.R. representative at my Mahá.

The implications of this swam like piranhas in my brain as I prepared to go to Sawyer's studio. We were slated to fill out the tracks compiled the day Heist died. Although I had recorded rough vocals at home, my fear at being around my colleagues now that I was Shimshana quickly replaced the anxiety resulting from Mom's revelation.

It had been over a week since I'd killed Heist with my voice. It was now under control, I hoped, but what about my hunger? I'd almost bitten Sawyer that same day. What if I killed again, just in a new way?

Just remember what I told you, Cici transmitted as I approached the door to the studio. *Stay hydrated. Stay calm. You can do this.*

Hydrated. Check. I took mental inventory of the ten thermoses of blood hidden in my knapsack.

Calm. Check…well not really. For breakfast, I'd gorged myself past the point of bloatedness. I wore my most comfortable pair of black jeans and a gold and white tee shirt. Nevertheless, I was nervous as all get out as I pressed my finger to the bell.

And for crying out loud, Angel, if you get hungry, leave as soon as possible.

I took a steadying breath as I listened to his footsteps approach before he opened the door. It wasn't Sawyer. It was a girl a little bit older than me with a no-nonsense attitude. And she smelled like chocolate. I used to love chocolate…

Hold your breath when they start smelling good to you.

The problem was, they all smelled good to me.

"You must be Angel," the older girl said. She gave me head-to-toe eye action before stepping aside for me to enter. "I'm Jackie. Sawyer's assistant."

Heist's replacement. As she disappeared into another room, I couldn't help thinking she had some giant shoes to fill. I picked up traces of Heist's scent. It was difficult to look at the soundboard and not remember his playful smile.

Seeing the others with my new immortal eyes was astounding. I noticed Sawyer's eyes had tiny red and gold flecks in them. He was thinner and his face was gaunt, as if he hadn't slept or eaten in days. His eyes caught my gaze and held it. "You seem different," he said.

I glanced at the spot where we had unsuccessfully tried to revive Heist. "I haven't been the same since that day."

His eyebrows drew together in that familiar frown and his wondrous scent dominated the room. I held my breath again. "Welcome back," was all he finally said.

Julietta burst into the studio. "Angel! I was worried about you. I wanted to come see you, but your Dad said you were too out of it for visitors. How are you?"

I offered all the perfunctory assurances of my recovery as LaLa entered, too. She glanced over at the spot where Heist died before hugging me. "You feel so warm," she said. "And you look a little...tired. You sure you're up to this?" I nodded, thinking it would be more accurate if she'd said "You look a little...immortal."

"Death, illness, and starvation," LaLa continued, emphasizing the word "starvation" with a pointed glance at Julietta's smaller frame. "We've seen them all this past week, and they can't stop us."

"Got that right," Julietta added.

"Let's do this," I said as we launched into working on the tracks.

Writing songs with the girls was always invigorating, but now that I was immortal, it was more intense than I thought it could ever be. It was like getting an injection of blood directly into my veins, as if the process of creating songs was like some sort of addictive drug. Not only could I see every note, I saw the various patterns that emerged when they came together. When the musical arrangement "worked," the patterns vibrated harmoniously. It actually felt like smooth, cool silk on my eyes as I watched the notes dance and vibrate around me. However, if the arrangement was off, not only was it as uncomfortable to look at as a scratchy wool sweater behind my eyelids, I could also see where in the arrangement the problem was.

Sawyer, eyebrows continually drawn together, listened to the playbacks of our lyrics along with his tracks. He nodded his head to the beat when something sounded right and remained still when it didn't quite work. If something was just plain wrong, he shook his head back and forth as if trying to toss the dysfunctional notes from his ears before leaning over the keyboard to rework the notes and chords.

One particular track, No. 6, was really giving the mortals a hard time. My eyes hurt looking into the places within the patterns where the disagreeable chords and notes were pulsating angrily. *I* could see exactly where the song wasn't working. But Sawyer couldn't.

I stepped toward the keyboard. "May I?" He scooted toward the lower octave end as I summoned my limited keyboard skills. Remembering the positioning of his fingers on the keys, I hesitantly pressed the notes that he'd just played. Yep, there it was. The chord that wasn't working. Ouch. He shook his head back and forth, and my eyes itched with the wrongness of the notes.

I closed my eyes and pictured that area working well. Incredibly, I saw the specific notes needed to bring the area into harmony. The needed notes were gray and floated outside of the pattern. All I had to do was choose which ones I wanted to use. But I moved too slowly. Sawyer had already slid his hand back over the keys and played the exact grayed-out notes I had just seen. Amazed, I watched the notes burst with color as they took their rightful place inside the pattern. The notes that weren't working went poof.

"That's it!" I cried. "That's what I saw!"

And then Sawyer smiled. I was floored.

His teeth flashed before my eyes as brightly as the notes. Somewhere in the back of my throat hunger arose, but it was diminished by the brilliance of the music. His hands had learned the new notes and played them automatically while he watched me intently. I couldn't take my eyes away from him. It felt like a blanket of magic had settled inside the studio and the two of us were wrapped up in it.

As we all continued working throughout the afternoon, I was even able to focus on the tasks at hand and ignore the distracting smells and sounds of being surrounded by mortals. It was still there tugging at my brain, but I managed to push it down. I sensed Cici's pride as I strengthened my resolve.

While we worked, Jackie attended to our every need and request. She wordlessly ran in and out for Sawyer's errands, as well as our lunch and snacks, and the never-ending requests for hot tea, lemon, and honey, which, to my surprise, I still wanted to drink. Every now and then I caught her glancing at me with a questioning look on her face.

I think she's interested in Sawyer and wondering what's going on between you guys.

Um, she shouldn't have to wonder very long, seeing as there's nothing going on between me and Sawyer.
Annoyed, I turned toward LaLa, only to find she smelled like honey. Drat. Did she always smell that good? I turned my back to her as my mouth started to water.

Go outside in the fresh air and break out a thermos.

I excused myself and concentrated on walking at a mortal's pace to the door. I oh-so-slowly reached out my hand to turn the lock to the open position before putting my hand on the knob. It amazed me how quickly I'd gotten used to flashing about here and there and going through solid objects. Now, the pace I'd moved at for sixteen years as a mortal was enough to put me to sleep. It helped to find

105

a rhythm between steps, like a jazz drumbeat. One Mississippi, two Mississippi...

Once I finally made it outside, I managed to drain one thermos before the door opened behind me. With a gust of fragrant, mortal air, Sawyer stepped out.

His eyes narrowed as he looked at me. "You okay?"

"Yeah," I answered. "Just needed a break."

He moved closer and my stomach tightened up. Would this continual craving to suck the blood out of everybody around me never end? Maybe Mom and Dad were right. Maybe I couldn't be around mortals anymore. Perhaps I should continue to write and perform in isolation. Or collaborate through some sort of software and meet up with them for gigs...

"I need your help," Sawyer was saying. I looked up at him. He didn't seem like the asking-for-help type. I waited for him to continue, and fought against becoming mesmerized by the way his Adam's apple slid up and down when he swallowed. "I need to buy a house," he continued. I looked at him blankly. "You said my apartment was soulless. (I didn't know he heard me tell Jules that!) You were right. And ever since Heist...I need a change. But I also need an honest opinion. Would you help me look? If you don't mind."

Huh? He asked me to go house shopping with him? "Why me?"

Yeah! I'd like to know, too.

"You're the only one I know here in Boston who tells me the whole truth. You don't seem to care whether you insult me or not."

"And you like that?"

"Yeah."

We stared at each other for a while. His eyelashes cast a shadow over his dilated pupils. The cold winter wind whipped his hair into his face.

"Sawyer, I know nothing about buying houses."

"Me, too."

"Well, okay, sure."

He smiled that self-deprecating half smile. "It's cold," he said.

"Yes," I agreed, and remembered I was standing outside in what was probably ten-degree wind chill in a tee shirt and jeans.

"No goose bumps?" He ran the ball of his thumb briefly along my forearm. A flash of what felt like fire race up my arm from where his hand made contact with my skin. The doorbell rang and I "ran" inside at a very slow, mortal pace to answer it. It was Nina.

She shook off her long wool coat. "Angel, glad you're back in the saddle. We've got only eight days to get choreography and costumes together for the Garden gig. Ladies, you more than likely have a number of loose ends to tie up from today's session, so I've brought the choreographer and designer to you."

And as if on cue, the bell rang again. A small, red-haired guy in tight white jeans floated in with what couldn't be described as less than a dancer's body. He sashayed about the studio as if he was about to break out into a routine à la "Fame," the TV series.

"Redd will teach you the moves," Nina said. "First rehearsal, tomorrow, Cambridge at the Dance Factory Studios," She consulted her Blackberry. "Three o'clock okay?"

Julietta was already picking up some simple steps with Redd. "Works for me," she said. LaLa and I agreed.

The bell rang again. A painfully thin girl stood at the door, and she seemed hesitant to come in until Sawyer invited her. "Risa," Nina said as an introduction. "She'll take care of the costumes."

Risa pulled out a tailor's measuring tape and started wrapping it around my bust. I self-consciously glanced in Sawyer's direction, but he was gone. I tuned in to hear him upstairs, rapidly breathing in and out and grunting. He was doing push-ups. With one part of my mind, I continued to listen to him and count along. Somewhere around push-up number seventy-eight, I turned my attention back to what Risa was doing. She rewarded me with a cutting glance as if she were insulted by my mental wanderings.

I felt guilty for eavesdropping on Sawyer and imagined what it would be like looking for a house with him. What was his taste in houses like? If this apartment/studio was any indication, we were in for some bland stuff.

Once we wrapped at the studio, LaLa made a beeline for the door with barely a nod in our direction. Julietta and I exchanged a sideways glance. Her haste could mean one of two things. Either she had some lyrics she desperately had to get down on paper in private, or there was a guy she had to talk to. I hoped it was the latter.

And what about you, Bighead? When's the last time you've even been out on a date? If LaLa found most guys unchallenging, I found them boring. After a few conversations, they always fell into one of three categories: obsessed with sex, obsessed with videogames, or obsessed with themselves. Or some boring combination of those. Even the smartest guys at school couldn't compete with a good song idea, a cup of tea, and a spanking-new pen to write with.

"What you got going on?" Julietta asked while picking up her knapsack.

"Doing Sawyer a favor. Helping him buy a new house."

"What!" she exclaimed in a whisper before pulling me to the side. Her eyes darted over to where Sawyer was now digging into album crates at the opposite end of the studio.

"Someone's got to help him," I said. "He asked me."

She seemed to think this was the most fascinating news since the death of Michael Jackson. "I want to know everything," she demanded in a whisper before heading out.

I turned to see Sawyer watching me with a small smile on his face. I felt irked. "What's so funny?"

"You look like a deer walking through a pride of lions," he teased. "Don't worry. I won't bite you."

I swallowed my impulse to warn him that he was the one in danger of being bitten.

16. SHOT TO THE HEART

To my surprise, Sawyer actually had good taste in houses.

He'd already identified the neighborhood he wanted to live in. The Back Bay was one of the most sought-after neighborhoods and boasted rows of high-priced brownstones alongside hip cafes, shops, and eateries. Sawyer's work on Swedish Moreno's number one smash, as well as a few minor hits for other artists, seemed to ensure money was no object for him.

We met his realtor, Sally, on the corner of Mass Ave. and Commonwealth. She was willowy, and despite her business attire, struck me like she'd be more comfortable in a long, flowered skirt and Birkenstocks. She pumped my hand. "Nice to meet you Angel. It must be nice to help your boyfriend look for his first home."

"No," I responded quickly. "I'm just a friend. Here for moral support."

Ha!

*Don't you have anything else to do besides eavesdrop
on all my conversations?*

Sally's knowing nod caused her hastily pulled together
bun to bob up and down on the nape of her veiny neck. She
proceeded to give us a brief rundown of the properties she
was about to show us. There were four in all and she was
positive they all met many, if not all, of Sawyer's
requirements. The main need was, of course, finding a good
layout to accommodate his home studio.

The first house had four stories. Sally gave us a tour of
the upper levels, which contained most of the five
bedrooms. We then stood on the entry-level looking out of
the French doors that lead to the back deck. Sawyer turned
to me. "What do you think?"

I took stock of the landscaped backyard and imagined
what kind of flowers bloomed there in the spring. "It's light
and airy," I replied.

"Yes, it is," Sally agreed. "And the lower level would
be perfect for your studio. It gets a good amount of natural
light and opens directly to the backyard.

"Let's take a look," Sawyer said. He descended a
couple steps before extending his hand to me. I refused to
take it. After all, why would I need help going down the
stairs? Hadn't I assured everyone I was recuperated? He
threw me an annoyed look from under his brows before
moving on through the space. There was a full bathroom
down there and a small kitchen.

"When they first built these houses, the popular thing
was to have the kitchen on the lower level," Sally said.
"Years later, the main kitchen was added to the entry-level
floor but the owners decided to keep the original kitchen
and rent out this level. You can get rid of it if you like."

I thought having a separate kitchen for the studio was
awesome and said as much. "That way you can stock it

with whatever your people need while working; water, tea, snacks."

Blood.

"See, that's why you're here," he remarked. "I'd have never thought of that." He raised his hand and touched the ceiling. "Ceiling's too low, though. I'd feel cramped."

You two might as well get married already, Angel.

Drop dead, Cici.

Sally flipped through the small mass of paper in her expandable folder. "We have three other properties. We can put this one on our short list, no pun intended, and go look at the next one."

She told us the second house was about a ten-minute walk away. Concentrating on walking at mortal speed, I matched my pace to Sawyer's and we ended up trailing behind her. "How long have you been writing music, Angel?" he asked in a casual tone.

"When I was really young, I'd hear melodies in my head and sing them out loud." I left out the part about remembering them note for note. "When I was about nine or ten, I started writing them down with lyrics."

"So you've been singing all your life."

We waited at the intersection for the light to turn pedestrian, and I turned to him. "According to Mom, I came out singing."

He was staring at me and didn't even try to look away. Or perhaps, like me, he was simply unable to look away. I breathed in, grateful to be surrounded by the myriad smells that ensured his aroma wasn't dominant, and therefore didn't drive me crazy. He guided me by the elbow as we started across the street.

You must not mate with him.

I nearly twisted my ankle in the middle of the intersection. Sawyer caught me in mid-trip, making sure I was steady before leading me to the curb and dropping his hand. Mortified, I tried to play it off. "Didn't see the little pothole." I glanced at him quickly. He had a small smile on his face. Probably because, clearly, there was no pothole. Confused, I took extra time straightening myself and looking down so I wouldn't see his mocking expression.

Cici, I'm not going to...mate with Sawyer.

Good. Because you could kill him if you did.

I gazed up at him, wanting to ignore this insane telepathic conversation. "And you? When did you know you wanted to do music?"

"I always knew." In response to a gust of wind, he hunched his shoulders and pulled his baseball cap further down on his head. "Music was my way of coping with reality. I grew up in...a less than ideal environment. If it weren't for music, I'd be a totally different person." I didn't realize I was hanging on his words until we caught up with Sally. She came to a stop.

"This area's had its share of foreclosures," she said. "In fact the next property's one of 'em."

"So we can probably get a good deal," I said. Sawyer glanced at me with an amused look.

"Yes. It's quite possible," Sally said. "As quiet as it's kept, it's still a buyer's market, even in this fancy neighborhood."

I became excited about the prospect of saving a few thousand on a house, even if it was someone else's money. During the Great Depression, Dad bought the brownstone next to our family's original house and knocked down the walls to create one large home. Seemed like his love for real estate had rubbed off on me.

Maybe you can buy your own soon. Fun, isn't it? She was right. It was fun.

Cici, what are you actually doing right now? I imagined her lounging in a cafe, sipping a lidded coffee cup full of warm blood and tuned into my escapades.

I'm in L.A. Sitting in Satchel's lap.

Alrighty then...that explained the turn of the conversation. My stomach growled.

Angel!

I know!

I glanced at Sawyer out of the corner of my eye, wondering how it would look if I broke out a thermos right there.

Sally led us into the next property. "How simply beautiful," I exclaimed loudly, as I slid a thermos into position within the secret compartment of my bag. "Wow, look at this sitting room," I bellowed while continuing on further into the house. I quickly took the thermos out, downed it, and put it back inside the bag before they made it into the room behind me.

As they walked in, I suctioned my teeth with my tongue to make sure all residue of blood was gone before turning to Sawyer. "Interesting wallpaper," I said. He grimaced at the pink rose-pattern on the walls.

Cici's laugh rang in my head. *You should go into acting.*

I feel like a fraud.

Welcome to immortal life in mortal territory. Just be glad you're too quick for them to see what you just did.

"You seem excited about this one," Sawyer said with a frown. "What is it you like?"

I felt like a fool for having underestimated him. I looked around the room. "The ceilings. If they're this tall on the entry level, they might be high enough downstairs. Higher than the last place, at least."

"Well, let's go see, shall we?" he said.

Downstairs, he reached up to touch the ceiling and couldn't. Sally pointed out the small kitchen and French doors opening out to the garden. "And we have a similar layout to the last property," she said. Sawyer seemed pleased as he prowled around the space.

And then I heard it. The sound of two human heartbeats up on the second floor. Deciding to investigate, I used the excuse of having to go to the bathroom.

"Need tissue?" Sally asked. "There may not be any in there."

"I have some in my bag thanks," I lied as I closed the door behind me.

When I heard Sawyer and Sally open the French doors and head into the backyard, I moved up the stairs in overdrive. I stood still in the hallway outside what must have been the master bedroom.

"Sounds like they're going in the backyard. I say we make a run for it," one voice said. It was female, and sounded almost elderly.

"But what if they see us, Ellie?" That was a male with a voice that sounded like he was around the same age as his friend.

I peeked around the corner. They were standing in the walk-in closet, and both wore large, hiker backpacks. The man closed up her backpack and secured it onto her back before pulling a handgun out of the outer pocket.

"Bill, we don't need that here. It's broad daylight and it's probably just another agent showing the place again."

"I'll keep it handy, just in case."

"Bill, we have to leave. It's not our home anymore."

"Like hell it ain't," he grumbled.

I stepped into the room. "What are you doing here?"

My intention was to scare them into leaving before Sawyer and Sally found out. But it didn't quite work out that way. I didn't count on Bill freaking out and shooting me. I watched the bullet enter my heart. *Good shot*, I thought as I felt the hot metal searing through the muscle. There were two possibilities before me. I could fall to the floor and play dead. Or I could give into the red rage threatening to grow in the wake of Bill's impulsive stupidity.

Don't kill them Angel! I fell to the floor and tried to figure out what to do next.

That's right, just lay there, bleed a little. And calm down.

Sawyer ran into the room. Bill dropped the gun to the floor and Sawyer kicked it away before catching sight of me. He exclaimed and staggered to his knees beside me while visibly trying to pull himself together. "Angel, you've been shot." He took my hand and the red haze cleared up. "Oh, my god," he said looking at the pool of blood I could feel expanding around me. Sally was calling 911, Ellie was apologizing and weeping, but I couldn't take my eyes off of Sawyer. For some reason, as I lay there looking up at his beautiful face, I wanted to cry, too.

He leaned over me and my eyes fluttered. The bullet began to move its way out as my body rejected it. Fascinating. It hurt like a bee sting more than anything else, but the loss of blood weakened me.

Dad's sending an ambulance. You'll have to work your way through this one until they get there.

Sawyer gave me water from his bottle. I coughed and spluttered as it went down my throat. "Easy," he said gently. There were tears in his eyes. "It looks like the bullet went right into your chest."

When the ambulance came, I recognized the drivers from the night of Heist's death. *Dad has a special arm of staff that deals with what they call immortal mishaps.* Sure enough, they took over, and covered up the bullet, now on the floor underneath me. One of the workers winked down at me. "You just take it easy, miss. You're lucky to be alive." They placed me on a stretcher.

The police arrived and took Bill into custody. "It was self defense," he cried as they led him away. "She just showed up in our bedroom."

"My blood's all over the floor," I told Sawyer before they wheeled me away. "Guess that means you'll have to buy this house."

17. THE TRUTH

"As far as everyone knows," Dad said in his matter-of-fact, doctor voice, "the bullet only grazed your chest and you are on track to a quick recovery."

I looked up at him from my hospital bed.

"The mortal who shot you is being handled by our police," Mom seethed. She was a livid shade of red, but thanks to Dad's glamour, no mortal could see it. "You will have to press charges, of course," she continued. "But all the details will be cleaned up."

"You have a visitor," Dad said.

The nurse entered. "There's a Sawyer Creed here to see Ms. Brown," she said.

Dad raised an eyebrow. "Are you up to it, Angel?" he asked. Ignoring the irony in his tone, I nodded to the nurse and soon Sawyer came in carrying a large bouquet of flowers that smelled almost as delectable as he did. Cici and Mom appreciatively inhaled both.

After greetings, Dad said, "Cleo, this is Sawyer Creed. He works with Angel. Sawyer, my wife Cleo."

"Nice to meet you, Mrs. Brown." Sawyer extended his hand to Mom.

I found myself holding my breath. Whenever Mom touched a person, especially for the first time, she was able to read them on the molecular level, as if she were running a person through an X-ray. Physically, there was very little you could hide from her. She clasped his hand. "Please call me Cleo, Sawyer." I could tell from her tone that something caught her attention. Cici and I exchanged a quick glance.

"How are you?" he asked me.

"Alive," I said. "The bullet just grazed my chest. Might even be home by tomorrow." He looked relieved and offered me the flowers.

Mom and Dad did their secret communication thing again.

They think he's your boyfriend, Cici thought. *So do I. Whatever.*

"Thanks." I took the flowers. "They're nice."

Hmmm, he's kind of sweet. In a hostile, mortal way.

"Mom, Dad," Cici said, "I think we should leave these two alone for a while." My face burned with embarrassment. What had gotten into my family? Sawyer must have thought they were insane.

Why did I even care what he thought?

"We'll see you later, dear," Mom said with a disapproving look. I sighed as they walked out the door.

"You're in pain." Sawyer said turning to me. "This is all my fault."

"How's that? How could you know there were gun-crazed squatters in there?"

He stepped closer to the bed, hesitated, and then sat down in the nearby chair. He peered up at me from under his ridiculously long eyelashes. His eyes watched my teeth

119

as they bit down on my lip in an effort to hold back the rush of words his presence evoked. I felt compelled to spill every secret, share every sensation, every new thing that had happened to me in the journey from fetus to adult, mortal to immortal. There was something about him that made me comfortable enough to be myself. With all the other mortals in my life I'd erected a friendly guard, but with him being guarded was difficult, as if he extracted the truth of me simply by being around.

"If I...hadn't asked you to come looking at houses," he said, "you wouldn't be here in the hospital."

"Well, maybe we should all just stay home and hide from all the messed-up random crap that can happen to us every day."

He looked at me like I was insane. And then he laughed. I nearly dropped my jaw. Who knew he was capable of laughing? Were his teeth always that straight? The corners of his eyes crinkled up and a dimple that wasn't there before popped up in his chin. I didn't realize how hard I was staring until he stopped. His smile faded and was replaced by the familiar frown.

"That's kind of what I do." His eyes locked with mine. "The studio's the safest place I know."

My temperature rose.

Angel, be cool. Literally. We don't want you to burn up your mortal boyfriend.

He's not my boyfriend! Burn him up...?

Yes, you can do it if you're not careful. You're still nowhere near being able to control yourself.

"It's kind of warm in here. Don't you think?" I said. "Would you crack the window?"

"Angel, it's freezing out there, and you're recuperating from what most would say's a shocking experience. Besides, a little heat doesn't bother me. I am from the South."

His eyes caressed me. My stomach flipped.

"But the question is," he continued in a serious tone, "will you be able to do the Garden gig like this?"

Now it was my turn to laugh. The idea of a bullet stopping me from doing anything, much less the gig of my life, was hysterical. "I'll tell you a little secret," I said when I was finally able to stop laughing. "Not even a bullet can stop me from getting on that stage. I'd have to drop dead before missing that gig, okay?"

And that really was the truth.

18. GLAMOUR

I tossed and turned all night in the hospital bed, but it wasn't due to pain. I just couldn't stop thinking about Sawyer Creed. I tried thinking about something, anything, else. That worked for a few seconds, until I was thinking about him again. Then I'd try again to think of something else, and the cycle continued around and around like a carousel. Eventually, I gave up trying to *not* think of him, and touched down in the bed after unknowingly hovering over it.

There were a number of reasons why Sawyer kept popping into my brain.

First: Mom gave me some information after she scanned him. Years ago, I'd asked her to not give me readings of my friends unless I asked for it. It was too creepy to know so much about a person while pretending you didn't. But with Sawyer, she gave her input whether I wanted it or not. I saw it coming as soon as she turned to me with the this-is-for-your-own-good glint in her eye.

"Honey, you should know I don't approve of your relationship with the producer. Both your father and I recommend sticking with our own kind for moral reasons." She looked at her fingernails while searching for the right words. "However. With some mortals the playing field is a little leveled. In these cases, the mortal is not an average mortal. There are many reasons for this, but usually it is genetic."

I had no idea what she meant. But it led me to the second reason I had Sawyer on my mind: I'd instinctively known there was something different about him, had felt it the first time I saw him and every subsequent time we were together. It was more than a North vs. South, Yankee vs. non-Yankee thing. There was something constantly working in his head. At first I'd written it off as the tendency music people have of always thinking of melody lines or being preoccupied with lyrics and arrangements. But it was more than that. There was something extra underneath that frown of concentration, and I wanted to know what that extra was.

Third reason: his vast musical knowledge exceeded my expectations. His passion for music matched mine, and when we worked together, it felt like we were the only people in the world. And the fourth reason I kept thinking about Sawyer was that I found him undeniably, immensely attractive. Watching him do anything—play the keyboard, talk, think, whatever—was fascinating. He'd mesmerized me before The Change, and now the fascination was even more intense.

These reasons, combined with his ability to bring the truth out of me, made our relationship dangerous. Not only because I wanted to tell him all my secrets, but also because the intense attraction might cause me to lose control and take his life.

Cici agreed with my conclusions the next day as we drove to The Nest. I listened to her insights anxiously while clutching Sawyer's flowers and another vase Jules and LaLa brought on their way from the choreography rehearsal I'd missed.

"Really, Angel," she said, "there's no way you can reveal who, and what, you are to him without putting him in danger." She politely waved another driver on and hung back as the other car merged into the traffic in front of us. "You can't have a real relationship without truth. The only mortals who know what we are are donors, and they're compelled." She came to a complete stop at the yellow light. I became impatient with the responsible speed at which we were traveling. I was starving. I zoned out on Cici and focused on not jumping out of the car to run the rest of the way. By the time we got there, Justin was already waiting.

Cici made her way over to the bar and I plopped myself down on our couch next to him. "You got here fast," I said, noticing his sweaty brow. I reached into the small tableside refrigerator and poured a glass of Gatorade for him. He quickly finished the drink, unbuttoned his shirt, and offered his neck. The muscles in his arms bulged more than last time and his natural scent mixed with the sweat smell. He put his hand on the timer, and that was all I needed. I pushed him back on the couch.

Afterwards, we sat with our arms wrapped around each other. I listened to his blood sing in my veins, and pondered the facts learned about him during this session. "You really love banana pudding that much?"

"I could love you more," he said in a low voice.

I froze in place. My head was on his shoulder, the place it always rested until we both calmed down from the feeding. But today he wasn't calming down; his heart was actually beating faster. And he was saying a word I couldn't wrap my head around. Love? Mom's warning about the inequity between Shimshana and their donors rang in my head. There was no way I could have a relationship with Justin, even though he was attractive, strong, honest, and the only mortal I didn't have to hide parts of myself from. I felt safe and comfortable with him. It would seem like the perfect match. But it could never be. He was a donor.

"Justin, I think you're suffering from something called Blood—"

"Don't patronize me, Angel," he interrupted. "Blood Obsession is one of the longest chapters in the donor textbook. I know all about it, and know it can drive you to do and say things you'd never do before the blood tie." He placed my hand in his and looked into my eyes. "But, I'm not suffering from it," he asserted, "and I always mean what I say."

He sunk his nose into my hair for a few seconds before leaving me to wonder if our blood tie was still a good idea.

"That's a no-brainer, sis," Cici said later as we made our way home. "I knew a girl who fell for her donor. She said it was like being in love with a loyal house pet. The deeper he got into her, the more he lost himself. They married and had one kid. Mortal. Now he and the kid are dead. Forty years later, she's still clinically depressed, was even hospitalized for a while after she'd driven herself crazy with guilt." She shook her head. "The Justin issue almost makes the Sawyer issue look hopeful. By the way, he called the hospital earlier when you were asleep. He wanted to know how your, ahem, injury was healing."

I was eager to call Sawyer back. After thinking about him all night (I'd finally fallen asleep around 4:19 a.m.), I had a ton of questions: what was his middle name? Did he have any brothers and sisters? How did he occupy his time when he wasn't making music? Did he miss Georgia? Did he even like Boston? Did he think about me as much as I thought about him? As Cici took the right turn at negative five miles per hour, I willed her to drive faster. *Safety first, Bighead.*

Once I was finally in the privacy of my room, I dialed Sawyer. As usual, he was in the studio. "Feel better?" he asked into the phone. One of our tracks played in the background.

"Nothing a Band Aid couldn't fix."

"I'm building out a track right now," he said. "Having a hard time. Can I come over for some vocals? I'll bring a portable recorder and you can sing into it. That is, if you're up to it."

"I'm fine. It's fine. Come on." I hung up. Whoa, I'd just invited Sawyer Creed to my house before asking permission. Anxiety caused me to float helplessly down the hallway.

"Breathe Angel, jeez," Cici said from the top of the stairs. I did, and came back to the floor.

"He's coming over to work on a track."

"No!"

"I know! I didn't even ask Mom and Dad."

"No, I'm saying you need to get ready. You look like a hot mess."

Mom was at the office. Down in the basement, Dad arched an eyebrow when I told him. "Angel, we always have an open-door policy for your friends. Just make sure you keep the door open to whatever room you two are in." He went back to the piece of furniture he was building.

Angel, come up quickly, Cici transmitted.

I raced up to her room, and was standing there before she finished the word "quickly."

"What's wrong?"

"Put these on," she said urgently while pressing clothes into my arms.

"I'm not getting dressed up. That's just lame."

"This is not dressing up. But to you anything that doesn't involve flannel, denim and/or fleece is formal. I'm just saying something a little bit more feminine might be in order."

"No," I repeated before jetting through the walls and back to my room to put on jeans and a designer t-shirt.

But, I did take time to attend to my hair. It grew thicker and faster since my change and now it surrounded my face like a zigzagged mass. Cici appeared behind me in the mirror.

"Help," was all I could say.

She immediately began, at an immortal speed, creating a French braid from the crown of my head to the nape of my neck. I sighed with the pleasure I always felt when Cici braided my hair. In a few seconds, the braid was done. I handed her a scrunchie. "You've got to be kidding," she said before tossing it in the wastebasket and disappearing.

She came back with a hair claw covered with pink crystals and intricate patterns. She affixed it onto the braid and transmitted what she saw so I could see the back of my head in my mind. "Pretty, right?" I nodded in agreement.

"Angel, have lunch before your guest arrives," Dad boomed from below.

I jetted through the floor to the kitchen and chucked down some stored Justin, which Mom had warmed for me before heading off to work. I went back to my room and sat on the bed to wait. It wasn't long before I heard his footsteps outside.

"Such confident footfalls," Cici joked from within her room. Dad cleared his throat in the basement before heading up to open the door.

I was confused, and unsure if I should wait until Dad called me, then casually saunter down to greet him, or go now and eagerly welcome him into our home.

This is what you do. Take a few extra seconds to check your makeup. Well, in your case, since you don't wear makeup, just make sure your face looks okay, there's nothing in your nose, no splatters of blood on your mouth, etc.

I looked in the mirror. I seemed a little too wild-eyed... Deep breath, and then another...

"Angel, your guest is here," Dad yelled.

By the time I made my way, mortally, down the stairs to the main level, Dad and Sawyer were sitting in the family room. Their conversation revolved around the Sox, the Celts, and the Pats. They both turned to me.

"Hi," I said while chewing the inside of my cheek.

Was it my imagination or did Sawyer's eyes light up? "Hi."

Dad tugged at his earlobe and scowled at us for a second. He then unfolded his long frame and headed back to his shop.

"You look like you were never in the hospital."

"Told you it was nada. Want something to drink?"

He accepted a bottle of mineral water before following me down the hall. I was aware of him quietly walking behind me as I entered the living room, and because I was embarrassed at what my eyes would give away, avoided his gaze for as long as I could. When I finally turned to face him, he was sitting at the grand, flipping through the sheet music on the stand.

"Pucinni. La Bohème," he read out loud. It was one of my favorite pieces, and was still unfolded on the stand as it had been since the last session with Mr. C.

"O Soave Fanciulla," I responded. "It's a duet."

"I know," he said. "It's my favorite opera."

I felt my face frown at his subtle admonishment, and felt guilty, yet again, for underestimating him. His fingers tinkled with the piano keys. And then he started to play.

And I could say nothing, do nothing except helplessly listen to him sing in a soft tenor:

"The dream that I see in you/
is the dream I'll always dream"

His voice was pop, but his pronunciation of the Italian was perfect. My knees trembled and I leaned against the piano for support. I joined him in the duet, my heart hammering against my ribcage like a songbird on fast-forward. My voice tailored itself to his and complemented his husky delivery.

The guy I'd once dismissed as a musical fraud was now in my home playing my heartstrings in a way I never knew could be so beautiful. He held my gaze through the rest of the song. The room glowed with the gorgeous notes, and there was nothing except music and him.

We reached the final notes, where he humbly deferred to me.

"Amore!"

I sang full out. His lips stretched into a smile as he pressed the final notes and watched me deliver the last vocals. The music came to a climatic end as his smile burned a brilliant pattern into my brain.

My feet were nowhere near the ground. He gasped, and abruptly stood up. We were almost face-to-face. "Wow," he whispered, wide-eyed, as he cupped my face in his hands and leaned his lips toward mine. As if in a dream, I breathed in his scent.

Angel!

My face fell when Dad appeared in the doorway behind Sawyer.

He's seen you levitate. Dad has to glamour him, Cici transmitted as Dad silently approached Sawyer from behind. *I'm so sorry, Angel.*

"No, Daddy!" Unwilling to watch, I turned away.

There was a brief silence, then I turned back around. Dad was gone, and Sawyer sat at the grand again, flipping through the sheet music as he had before.

It was as if the duet never happened.

"Perhaps we should get started on the track," he said, seemingly unaware of the magic that had happened between us just minutes ago and how it changed my life forever. I nodded and refused to cry, since surely the sight of my bloody tears would warrant another glamouring.

We went to work. I sang a few takes as he played the track. As soon as he recorded what he needed, he rose to leave. His brow knitted into a frown as he tersely thanked me for my time.

Cici squatted next to where I had thrown myself on the floor after closing the door behind Sawyer. "Don't make that mistake again, sis. Forget about him."

She reached out to comfort me, but I pushed her hand away and pressed my lips together to swallow the devastating sound rising up from my shattered heart.

19. THE GARDEN

Since I was the one "recovering," the girls came over to my house a couple times to work on the tracks, teach me Redd's choreography, and practice the song we were going to perform at the Garden gig. Although we had performed "Get Out Of Here" numerous times over the past year, Julietta had some ideas for adding spice to the existing harmonies. Thanks to Mr. C.'s "love" technique, the passionate emotions the song always evoked in me were channeled through my voice, and seemed to affect the girls, too. As a result, our collective delivery sounded better than ever.

After rehearsing, we were sprawled about the family room writing lyrics, and drinking tea and hot chocolate. A fire roared in the fireplace, and outside, the snow was coming down in a torrent. Mom called from the kitchen. "Would you girls like some cookies?"

"Yes!" they yelled back enthusiastically. They always loved Mom's holiday cookies. I, on the other hand, would never again enjoy those miniature snowmen, reindeer, and elves.

"Mmmm…so good," LaLa said as she dunked one into the hot chocolate. I watched her, jealously sipping my "hot chocolate" which really wasn't hot chocolate at all. Cici had finally perfected a drink glamour that allowed me to drink blood that looked and smelled to mortals like anything I announced it to be. Dad deemed it brilliant.

"I'm not going to eat anything else today," Julietta said as she stuffed another cookie into her mouth. She was back on her diet.

"Girl, you better stop that crazy bulimia thing or you'll end up with osteoporosis," LaLa said with crumbs flying out of her mouth.

"Whatever. Did he really take the blame for you getting shot?" Julietta asked me.

They both waited for an answer.

"He said it was because he'd asked me to look at houses with him." Their eyes opened wide before they burst into giggles.

"Has he kissed you yet?" LaLa probed.

Weird. That was the sort of thing Julietta would ask. I felt my face frown. "It's not like that."

"Yeah, right," Julietta said with an uncharacteristically cynical tone.

The idea of kissing Sawyer was almost too much to bear. To be so close to him, to actually taste him…the thought alone was almost enough to send me over the edge. I bit into a cookie. It tasted like what I imagined kitty litter might, but it distracted me from fantasizing about tasting Sawyer. Masochistically, I continued to chew.

###

Days later not even our annual family Christmas activities could take my mind off of kissing Sawyer. While we shopped for and decorated the tree, the idea of what would happen if I ever got that close to him tormented me. Singing happy carols couldn't make me forget that I'd literally eat him alive.

Our first family ski break of the year, scheduled earlier to accommodate the weekend's Garden gig, couldn't take away the dreadful thoughts. You'd think I'd be enjoying my new immortal prowess on the slopes, but no. All I could think about was whether Sawyer liked to ski. I was obsessed. Mom and Dad kept looking at me as if I'd lost my mind. Cici's telepathic silence on the topic was louder than an "I told you so." They all knew what I knew. That if I'd manage to keep Sawyer alive after the first taste, there would be no hope of him living much longer.

These thoughts were still in the back of my mind a couple days later when the stretch Hummer, sent by Quake Records, showed up at the door.

"Sure beats the Green Line," LaLa said, referring to Boston's mass transit system. She ran her hands over the leather seats. There was a pop-music mix pumping through the speakers, and we hummed along to the tunes to warm up our vocal chords. It was more of an attempt, on my part, to continue to look "normal" since I no longer needed to warm up. My voice was now capable of going from zero to one-sixty in a matter of seconds.

Julietta, the first to get picked up, nursed a cup of hot water and lemon. She pointed to the hot water dispenser, and I leaned forward to fix myself a cup before locating some honey, stirring and staring out the window at the city. Outside, a fresh top layer of snow was being whipped into

mini tornadoes by gusts of freezing wind; a quantum leap
from the vehicle's warm luxury.

I caught the look of disbelief on LaLa's face. "It's like a
too-good-to-be-true dream," she said, gesturing to our
surroundings. "One part of my mind says something bad's
going to happen."

"Yep," Jules chimed in. "It's surreal. But we worked
for this. It's been four years and a thousand gigs. And did
we rock rehearsal or what?"

Earlier, we had a technical rehearsal on the Garden
stage. And the effect my emotions had on others while
singing, what I had sensed during my rehearsals with the
girls, was confirmed. I'd felt excited. Excited about being
in control of my voice, excited to be on the stage, and
excited just to be alive. Through my voice, my excitement
was transferred to everyone around me—stagehands,
producers, stage managers, assistants, the girls; everybody
was amped up, too.

This confirmation made me wonder, though…were
Sawyer's feelings during our duet real…or a result of
transferring my own emotions through my voice?

I still pondered that question as the Hummer pulled
into the backstage entrance to the Garden. Nina, dressed in
a sharp black suit and heels, waited by the entrance. She led
us through a maze of corridors and access-restricted areas
until we got to our dressing room.

It was two hours before we were due on stage. Nina
left us to our own devices, promising she'd see us backstage
after we were done. We hardly noticed she'd left because
the sight of our outfits took all our attention.

They were awesome.

All three were silver, pink and white, but each one
reflected the personality of the wearer. LaLa's consisted of
skin-tight pants, a tank, and a glistening baseball cap, while
both Jules and I got miniskirts. I got stilettos and angel

wings and Jules had the knee-high platform boots and beaded headgear. I sashayed around with the wings on. They were surprisingly comfortable. "Good," stone-faced Risa said, detaching the wings to allow me to sit for makeup and hair.

"Not so good," LaLa said as we all took in the way Jules' outfit hung on her.

"How much weight did you lose this time?" I asked. Julietta looked down at her body as if she was seeing it for the first time.

"About twelve pounds," she answered.

As LaLa and I voiced our disapproval of Jules' crash-dieting, an emotionless Risa sat down at her portable sewing machine and started taking in material without a word. Meanwhile, we practiced our harmonies until the makeup artist kept our lips too busy. The hairstylist worked until my face, neck, and shoulders were framed by a mass of silky spirals. Soon, Julietta's costume was ready. I didn't know much about sewing, but was impressed by Risa's quickness with the alterations. Jules' outfit fit her perfectly.

We oohed and aahed at the transformation of Kat Trio. We'd dressed up for gigs before but never at this level. I loved the look of the eyelashes and rhinestones on my eyes.

"So pretty," Jules gushed. "We look hot!"

"Yeah, I hope you're able to dance in those," LaLa said pointing to our shoes. Quickly, Julietta and I reviewed the choreography to get acclimated to the shoes. It was a shaky start, but soon we were able to dance normally. And then we were ready to go. At least on the outside. But on the inside I was a ball of nerves.

Relax, Angel. I'm in the audience. Guess who's with me?"

I sniffed the air. Mom and Dad! *That's supposed to make me feel relaxed?*

I remembered not too long ago wishing Mom and Dad could see me perform again, but the thought of it happening tonight made me more nervous. After all, my family hadn't seen me perform for two years. What if they didn't like the way my performance style had evolved? What if they thought I was wasting my time and should focus more on school?

They're not here to judge you. They're here to make sure you don't kill anybody.

Even worse. I had images of Mom or Dad trying to explain to the police how their daughter decimated a crowd of thousands with her voice. I felt myself lift out of my chair.

Angel Brown, get a hold of yourself right now before I come back there! You're getting all worked up and we can't have that tonight.

She was right. I took a deep breath and felt myself settle firmly back into my chair. There was a knock on the door. "Who's there?" I called out while taking another quick look in the mirror. His scent had already answered my question.

"Are you decent?" Sawyer said from behind the door.

"Angel's butt naked, so come on in!" LaLa yelled.

The door opened, and in walked Sawyer surrounded by his aroma. Overcome with emotion, I struggled to look preoccupied with getting my wings re-attached and avoided his gaze. He couldn't remember what happened at the house, and his reaction before the glamour was probably only a result of my new singing technique. There was no way he felt about me the way I felt about him.

He caught my eye briefly in the mirror and my temperature rose. *Angel, chill out!* I took a deep breath and visualized polar ice caps.

After some general small talk about the tracks we were working on, and talk of breaking our collective leg, he walked over to where I stood. "How do you feel?" he asked. His tone and demeanor seemed more intimate than before. Yet, if I told him how I really felt, it would all be over.

"Like everything's changed." Drat, I had to keep it light; there was no need to go all General Hospital on him. But it was impossible to keep up a carefree pretense when all I wanted to do was hear him sing again and drown in his arms.

His heartbeat sped up but he didn't say anything. He only looked at me hard and long before turning on his heel and walking out.

LaLa took in my reaction. "You okay, Angel?"

"Yes, doggone it, I'm okay. When do we start?" There was dead silence for a few seconds before both LaLa and Julietta broke out into gales of laughter. I realized how ridiculous my response had been and laughed, too, in an effort to shake off the Sawyer effect.

Another knock at the door.

It was the stage manager, telling us it was time to go to the stage. We clasped hands and bowed our heads while LaLa quickly mouthed words of inspiration and encouragement. As usual it lifted my spirits, but this time as she spoke the name of Jesus, I couldn't help but imagine him as a small, hunted boy attending Mom's Mahá.

As we were led to the stage, every detail of everything around me came into hyper-focus, down to the rivets in the concrete walls. I'd never been so alert. So ready to sing. So scared. It felt as if my feet weren't touching the floor as we walked on.

They're not Angel. Dad's got glamour action going on so no one notices. I can't wait until you get out on the stage! I always wondered how it felt to be in front of an audience, and now I'll get to feel it through you.

Just consider me your living porthole into Angel-ville.

We finally arrived at the stage's wings. There were a number of people there, but Charmain, the main act, was nowhere to be seen. I imagined her in an elaborately appointed dressing room, eating Godiva and sipping Cristal champagne with her entourage.

The stage manager pointed toward the narrow passage leading to the stage. "Wait here until they intro you and then you'll go though this way. You've got fifteen minutes."

"Oh my god," Julietta said as she peeked out at the audience. "There's a million people out there."

"A little more than fourteen thousand, to be exact" said a friendly-looking girl dressed in super-tight jeans and combat boots. "It's sold out. I'm Joy. Bass player. Elio."

Of course. Elio was one of our favorite bands and we were almost as excited to be sharing a stage with them as Charmain. They were funky, edgy, and despite being unpredictable in their musical style, had managed to get a Top 20 hit that rocked the clubs, too. We met the rest of the band members, and we all tamed our nerves by joking and discussing everything except the reason why we were there.

Soon, we heard the applause as our backup band took the stage. We got into position. Over the loudspeaker we heard: "Ladies and Gentlemen. Introducing Kat Trio."

With whispered wishes of "break a leg," everyone melted away from us as we fell into our choreographed, slinky entrance onto the stage. After a four-beat pause where we stood frozen on the stage in various poses, we broke into a sequence of Redd's sexy, leggy moves while the band played an extended intro.

With my new immortal eyes, I easily saw the audience beyond the bright footlights that had always blinded me in the past. So many people! And they were really clapping for us! On the beat where we kicked our legs out, the three of us took our concentration away from the choreography just long enough to flash smiles at one another. Knowing all these people were even remotely interested in our work sent shivers down my spine.

I saw Mom, Dad, and Cici to my left, toward the front. I saw Sawyer sitting in the front row surrounded by other members of the music industry insiders' club, including Raj. Nina sat with them, watching our every move, no doubt taking notes. A whole host of local artists were in attendance; some, we'd met through the years, some we'd beaten at competitions. I even saw classmates from school.

Beneath everything was the steady clatter of mortal movements, breathing, activity, and heartbeats. I took a deep breath and inhaled the epic aroma of mortality. Ahhhhhh...

And then I saw her.

She was sitting in the fourth row, sixty-eight people in from the right. It was the lady my reflection had morphed into. She was smiling at me, and it was the most frightening thing I'd ever seen. It was less a smile than a baring of teeth. She may have been alone, or she could have been sitting with a hundred other anomalies. I couldn't tell because she alone had my complete attention.

She had no heartbeat.

Whoa, Angel. Calm down. Dad's working harder so whatever just happened, let it go.

Cici could pick up on my thoughts and feelings, but for some reason she couldn't see I was responding to the Lady in the audience. The Lady who could somehow shield my perception of her from Cici and Dad's telepathy. In the minute it took me to register all of this, the intro choreography wound down and the musical cue came for us to start singing. Despite my success with Mr. C.'s technique, I quickly offered up a silent prayer to not kill anyone with my voice before we broke into the opening line of "Get Out of Here:"

`"Motorcycle, boat, jet/`

> *Helicopter, corvette.*
> *I just gotta get out of here."*

Some sections of the crowd went wild. There were comments ranging from "Who the hell are they?" to "I knew them back in the day, before they blew up" to "This is my favorite Kat Trio song!" In my mortal life it took all of my concentration to execute a song just right, but now I could do it while simultaneously taking in a ton of additional information. Some of the comments from a lot of guys, and a few girls, were focused on our costumes: what was underneath them and the body parts exposed or not exposed. Gross. I made a mental note to block out this type of X-rated chatter from the audience.

I watched the sound waves bounce off the back walls of the Garden and ricochet to the front. The colors glowed in the darkness beyond the stage, mingled with the lights emanating from hundreds of cell phones, and then gently dissolved into the air. After a while, I missed the mortal feeling of concentrating solely on the song and decided to block out everything superfluous. I closed my eyes and lost myself in the music.

And then there was no sound. No music. No heartbeats. There was nothing at all. I opened my eyes. The band seemed frozen. Julietta, LaLa, the audience, even Mom and Dad. Nobody moved.

"Mom?" I reached toward her, but she seemed frozen. My voice sounded as if I were in a weird echo chamber. "Dad?" Same response. *Cici!* I listened. Nothing.

What was going on? Why was I the only one capable of moving or, apparently, thinking? Then it occurred to me. I did this. Dad said it took a year for abilities to solidify, and here was an ability I didn't even know I possessed.

Somehow, in my desire to fully connect with the music, I had *un-connected* everybody from the flow of time.

20. THE LADY

The entire audience, and everyone I loved, was frozen in time and I wasn't sure how I did it. Even worse, I didn't know how to get things back to normal.

Mom, Dad, and Cici, frozen along with everyone else, weren't able to help me out of this one. How could I undo something I didn't even know how I did in the first place?

"If you get any higher off the stage, you'll be flying." The Lady, immune to what was happening, calmly surveyed the scene. "This is your doing," she continued. "You possess power you are not even aware of." She laughed then. Hysterically. As if she were sitting front row at a comedy club.

I wanted to tell her to stop laughing and shut up, but my sense of self-preservation kept my own mouth closed. I didn't even know *what* she was. All I knew was she had no heartbeat, yet somehow lived. She was now an individual, separate from me and immune to my influence, and seemingly immune to my family's powers. "How do I know you're not responsible for this?"

"It's all you, Angel."

"What are you?"

"A part of you."

She smiled again. I wanted to punch her teeth down her throat.

"You've got a terrible temper. You're very close to sending this place up in flames." She glanced suggestively at my family.

"Leave them alone." My hands clenched painfully as I stared at her with hot, angry eyes.

"When the Council finds out about this interesting power you have, it'll get downright dangerous for you. They might want to kill you."

"Is that a threat?"

"To put it in a cliché human way, that's a fact." It didn't escape my attention that she implied she was not human. Turning her face away from me slowly, she pointed to three individuals scattered about the room. They, too, were frozen. Were they Council members? The Lady nodded as if she heard my thought. "A newborn onstage before all these mortals. Of course they came to see firsthand. I think I will help them figure it out."

She reached her hands out to the three Council members, and in the blink of an eye, performed a movement that unfroze them and them alone. In a flash, she returned to her seat in the audience and sat completely still before any of them saw her. I gasped at her audacity.

Like gophers in a strange landscape, the Council members scrutinized the Garden, then each other and then, finally, me. I recognized one of them; Charleston, the black-eyed man from Mom's office. I could only guess what they were thinking. They gawked at Mom and then back at me in astonishment. I had to get things back to normal. I didn't know how to, but I had to figure out how to fix it. Fast.

I supposed the first move was to calm down. I took a few deep breaths and, afterward, noticed air particles starting to move, but still not enough to get things back to normal. I concentrated on the air particles, willed them back into circulation. Concentrating on the fourteen thousand plus people in the room, mortal and immortal, I willed them to move, to breathe, to become animated once more. And they did. As if they'd never stopped. They didn't even know what had happened. I picked up the exact note that emanated from my mouth the moment before everything went screwy.

The Council Members looked around in amazement. I shut my mind down. I'd tell Cici later, but for now I had to keep this to myself until I understood what happened. And, I would have to tell Mom. For her to hear it from the Council first would be disastrous. Her commitment to the Council was an ancient bond that seemed to surpass even her commitment to me. How could she defend me when I didn't even know what I was capable of doing?

As we performed the closing chorus, I heard the roar of the crowd, but I couldn't enjoy the appreciation. The Lady flashed that eerie smile and clapped her hands with an exaggerated cadence. I realized she'd set me up. My vocal tones of love quickly turned to tones of outrage. I extended the vengeful notes into an impromptu solo. The dark beyond the footlights turned bloody red black, and the roar of the crowd turned to frenzied screams. Scuffles and yelling broke out in various areas around the Garden. Angry exchanges mixed with the dull sounds of fists pounding on flesh. I sensed Jules and LaLa's confusion. The band desperately tried to cover this unrehearsed extension of the song even as their playing grew more aggressive and driving.

The Garden and our music had quickly descended to the brink of chaos in response to the angry notes coming from my mouth. And, in the midst of it all, the Lady sat. She glanced pointedly at Mom who stared at me with an eerie gaze. Her face seemed carved from stone, and her eyes were unreadable. A chill went up my spine.

Cici confirmed what I'd suspected. *Mom's considering shutting you down by taking molecules out of your brain. The way she did Tunde.*

I refused to let the Lady succeed in destroying my family. I willed myself to feel the calming energy emanating from Cici and Dad as they worked to bring my anger level down. I allowed myself to relax back into the loving space Mr. C. instilled in me and ended the song on a note of bliss. The applause was deafening and continued long after we'd left the stage.

Backstage, Elio members regarded us in awe as the crowd continued to chant our name under their introduction. Bravely, Joy and her fellow band members went out to the stage despite the fact the crowd still clamored for us.

Nina rushed toward us. "What was that at the end? When did you rehearse that?"

LaLa glared at me. "We didn't," she said pointedly.

"Doesn't seem to matter, does it?" Jules said to me. "It's always about Angel."

"I'm really sorry." I scrambled for the right words. "I got carried away." It was a lame explanation but I didn't know what else to say.

"Last time I checked," LaLa continued, "Kat *Trio* wasn't a solo act."

That hurt. It seemed as if everything the three of us had built together was falling apart, and from the looks of what went down on stage, it could only get worse. I'd worked so hard not to kill anyone with my voice, but ended up freezing everyone with it. There was no hope for me. The girls' reactions were nothing compared to what I was about to face from Mom, not to mention the Council. I was done.

I threw up my hands in resignation and turned back to Nina. I was ready to quit. But before I could tell her to kick me out of the group, Nina smiled ear-to-ear. "Whatever that was, Angel, you better keep doing it, because I've never seen a crowd react like that in my entire career."

Jules started to say something, and then backed down as Nina continued to rave. "The crowd literally went ballistic with that solo. I guarantee you the papers will have stellar reviews tomorrow."

One by one the members of our backup band came up and shook my hand. I heard myself thanking them for being on their toes and going with the flow. LaLa turned away, and the look on Julietta's face said it all.

She looked betrayed.

A girl ran up to me. "You Angel?" she asked breathlessly. Her heart hammered as if she'd run at top speed to get to me.

"Who're you?" I asked.

"I work for Charmain. She's asking you to her after-show party."

"Me? What about my partners?"

"She just said you."

"No thanks. Not without them." I tossed the words over my shoulder before turning my back to her. I caught Julietta's look and it brought back every memory we shared, every gig, every dream we revealed to each other, every defeat and embarrassment we'd ever suffered. She wrapped her arms around me and I took in her sweet, delicious smell and hugged her back as hard as I could without hurting her. LaLa wrapped her long arms around the both of us and we stayed like that for a while. I knew I'd have to pull away before my instincts got the better of me but for now, just for a few brief seconds, I reveled in our bond.

A frenzied voice caught my attention. Down the hall, hundreds of feet away in the green room, Raj frantically called the car service and begged them to send the Hummer back to collect us. The label execs had changed their minds, he explained, and were now willing to pay more for the "new girls" now there was apparent star potential.

So, before the audience erupted into pandemonium, the execs were okay with us finding our own way back home. I held back a cynical snicker. Like Nina, the label execs saw dollar signs in an audience manipulated from one side of the emotional spectrum to the other. They didn't understand the nature of the manipulation, but it didn't matter. As far as they were concerned, the results in the crowd could be translated into sales. Soon they surrounded us, smiling and circling like sharks smelling blood in the water. They shook Nina's hand while regarding us with flashing teeth. I hugged my girls closer and wondered who was scarier, the mortals or the immortals.

The sight of Dad, Mom, and Cici striding toward me answered that naive question right away. I excused myself and walked with my family to an empty side hallway off the main corridor. Cici handed me a thermos. I drank and opened my mind to allow her to see everything that happened while I was on stage. Seconds later, Dad joined my sister in gawking at me as if I'd just committed a terrorist act.

Mom was the odd man out. "What?" she asked. All she had to go on were the looks on our faces to know something massive had happened. Dad whispered rapidly in her ear. Her face registered bewilderment. "How do you know they were Council members and why were they the only ones not affected by the time freeze?" she asked.

I couldn't say why. I literally couldn't speak the words or show them with my thoughts anything that had to do with the Lady. It was as if there was a spell on me that prevented me from talking about her. "I can't say," I answered.

Mom exhaled and then squared her shoulders with an air of resolution. "Your Mahá is now more crucial and we must start it as soon as possible," she answered. "If, at your Mahá, you are branded a threat, the verdict will be passed. There would be nothing I can do to save you. For now, I will do damage control to stop the momentum of backlash that is sure to be brewing as we speak."

And with that she disappeared. All I could do was gulp.

"This is grave news," Dad said to me in a gentle tone, "and I am sorry you are hearing this on what should be one of the best nights of your life."

"She reversed the freeze!" Cici's voice sounded an octave higher than usual. "That must count for something in her favor." He sadly shook his head "no."

"What is most frustrating is we cannot assist you with this," he said. "You will have to reign it in on your own so that your Mahá will find you able to turn it on and off at will. Otherwise, the consequences will be death for you. And possibly us for aiding and abetting."

I felt sick. After all that we had been through, I ended up putting my family at risk anyway, and in a worse way than I could ever imagine. Was there no one who could help me? Help us?

"Mahá will last about five to seven mortal days," Dad said. "Unfortunately, you'll have to be absent from school." Well, at least there was *some* light in this tunnel. "We'll tell everyone that you're on a family trip," he added. "One designed to give you a chance to rest after all the excitement you have had recently."

"Great, everyone's going to think I had a nervous breakdown."

"It'll explain that scary solo," Cici pointed out.

Whatever. I didn't want Mahá; I just wanted to work on the tracks and see Sawyer again. But now it looked like I might die before getting a chance to do either. Through a red haze, I swore that if I saw the Lady again, I'd be ready to use my power to protect my family and put an end to her threat.

21. MAHÁ

The next morning we were at the Mahá house. "*Your house,*" Cici reminded me. We were sitting on the double-spiral staircase that opened to the grand foyer. I looked around, still amazed. With twenty-six bedrooms and Victorian architectural details, including a tower and turrets, it was more a mansion than a house.

Mom stood with PE's Head of Decor and watched a couple of the mortal employees hang an enormous, cross-like object above the main entrance. I looked to Cici. *That's the Yah. The official living symbol of our house as law for this Mahá. It's a scary ancient thing. If a guest breaks the Law of the Mahá house, it's the same as dissing the Yah. If you diss the Yah, it can somehow kill you with permission from the owner of the house.*

Diss the Yah. Die. Got it.

Nearby, Dad was talking in Mandarin to an immaculately dressed Asian woman. "Who's that?" I asked.

"An old friend of Dad's and your personal stylist for the Mahá. She'll make sure your makeup, jewelry, scent, hair will be perfect."

A girl about my age bounced over, carrying a makeup case. "I'm Demeter, your makeup artist!" she trilled.

"Hi…"

"I'm your biggest fan!" She smiled widely, as if she wanted to say more, but Mandarin Woman laid a hand on her arm. "Well, nice meeting you, Angelica!" she said before being led away.

"RoRo!" Cici yelled suddenly. Without thinking, she flew out the door. The mortals in the room stood dumbfounded at what they'd just witnessed. Dad nodded at his apprentice Eric, who rapidly went to each one and touched them with a crooked wand I call "the erase stick." As soon as I knew they had all forgotten what happened during the last one or two minutes, I went down to greet my oldest sister.

Of all of us, Aurora was probably the most aptly named. Her personal radiance competed with the sunlight streaming through the windows. Her smile was brilliant as she rushed to hug everyone. Her waist-length beaded braids jingled like bells as she stroked my hair and face. "You have grown so beautifully," she said in a perfect, formal European accent. Her mate, Roman (they didn't use the mortal terms of husband and wife) came in, carrying their suitcases. He was one of those chilly vampires that walk in the sunlight.

Technically, he didn't have to be here, since Mahá is just for natural-born immortals, but he and Aurora never traveled apart from each other if they didn't have to. He was protective of her, and drawn by her innate warmth. She was addicted to his particular type of wildness and cold, deadly nature. It was a match made in heaven. He greeted us all with his thick Russian accent.

Suddenly, I was forcefully pushed from behind. Taken off-guard, I forgot Mom's charm-school lesson and broke into a low snarl as I whipped around.

Nobody was there...but there was the faint outline of a tall, masculine person...

"Adrian, cut it out," Cici chided.

My brother appeared out of invisible mode. "Idiot!" I said, hugging his massive frame. He was my only non-Shimshana sibling, but he could change into any existing animal he wanted. At five hundred and eighty-one years of age, he was also still single, probably because he'd just returned from spending the last seventy years living as a turtle.

My oldest siblings, twin brothers Menelik and Memnon, arrived wrapped in flowing black robes. Silent and sullen, they looked as if they still lived in another millennium. I had met them briefly as a baby and now, at one thousand, eight hundred fifty-one years of age, they looked exactly the same as they had then. They moved as one person, and although they themselves were telepathically linked, they were not telepaths. They both knelt at Mom's feet.

"D'qatsmaa Aemeh," they said in stereo.

Aramaic for "divine mother." They're stuck in the past. They were traumatized when Tunde killed their Dad.

Their eyes rested on me. "Um, hi," I said awkwardly.

"Hi," they repeated the word back before they turned to look at each other with what looked like astonishment.

"I designed a family wing for us," Cici told everyone. "Staff will help you settle in. The commencement ritual starts in an hour." The staff hustled their luggage away to the service elevator and led them all up the main staircase.

Cici turned to me. "And as for you, it's time you got ready." With that, she guided me to my private suite.

It was huge. A panel of windows and French doors faced the east and overlooked the Pacific Ocean. The bed was a canopy style (I'd always wanted one of those) with a wrought iron headboard featuring vines and angel faces. It was very elaborate, like something I'd seen on TV, and all the bedding was white and fluffy. There was an altar along the western wall, it was enclosed in an intricately carved cabinet that now had its doors flung open.

"Whoa," was all I could say. Cici held herself proudly as I explored the room. It was three times the size of my bedroom at home. A small row of high, cross-shaped portholes let in natural light and fresh sea air. But it was the collection of clothes that knocked me for a loop. In the equally large dressing room, one entire wall was nothing but shoes from top to bottom. Attached to the walls were sliding ladders for easy access to the upper shelves.

"They're separated by color and function," Cici offered. "You've got your kicks here, heels, flip-flops for the beach party, slides...This wall over here is all ceremonial and ritual gear."

There were long flowing traditional garments and capes. One in particular caught my eye, and I recognized the midnight blue fabric Mom had picked out. I ran my hand along its exquisite purple, gold, and silver embroidery. There was even a section of jewelry, and some of it looked very old. Amulets, headdresses, bracelets, rings, necklaces. My head was spinning.

"This wall over here is non-ceremonial clothing," Cici said while pointing to sections with dresses, drawers full of cool comfortable underthings, bikinis, t-shirts, shorts, skirts.

"I feel like I'm in a store. Am I really going to wear all this stuff?"

"You're sure gonna try," Cici said while pulling out a white dress. "Jump in the shower. There's a special soap in there. Make sure the water's really hot to open up your pores."

The bathroom had a ginormous window overlooking the ocean and a tub that was big enough for a small family. Marble was everywhere, and candles were lighted, despite the time of day. I inhaled the soothing aroma of burning sage and stepped into the double shower. The soap—some sort of homemade herbal concoction—smelled amazing, and I breathed in the relaxing scent. When I was done, I dried off and went back into the dressing room.

Cici, Aurora, and Mom were there, all in white sheath dresses that flowed down to just above their ankles. They were all barefoot. Opera lilted through the suite via strategically placed wireless speakers. Incense wafted through the air.

Mom first rubbed me down with oils from pretty, colored glass bottles, then handed me my dress, a red bra, and red panties. "The red undergarments represent the life force, the blood," she explained. "White is the new beginning that is your immortal life."

"I'll do your makeup," Aurora said as she readied a pot of black for my eyes. Meanwhile, Cici started styling my hair. I closed my eyes and concentrated on my breathing.

"There is no need to panic, Angel," Aurora reassured. "This ritual will just be us. All of your immediate family members. It is the first ceremony that will open the door for the Mahá. It hasn't changed since Mom's Mahá. Except, perhaps, they did not have red thongs back then."

I heard the smile in her voice and imagined Mom's glance. I giggled softly, or at least as much as I could while she applied lip liner. Soon they were finished with their administrations. I opened my eyes. Cici flipped a switch and the part of the wall that was covered with black velvet rolled back to reveal a wall-length mirror. The mirror was set in a simple, yet elegant, gold frame. At the top was the head of Hathor, the Egyptian goddess of fertility and beauty. But it was my reflection that startled me. I looked like an ancient Egyptian princess.

Mom tied a red sash around my waist. Cici attached something that looked like a tiny garter belt to my right upper arm. The belt sported a pouch, into which Aurora placed a small dagger. "At the end of our ritual," Cici said, "you'll slit your wrist and allow seven drops of blood into the goblet."

"Why seven?"

"You are my seventh child," Mom said.

She placed an amulet around my neck. Hung on a thin gold chain, it was breathtaking in its detail. It depicted a pyramid before a rising sun, a falcon with outstretched wings and the head of a lion. There were ancient Nubian words inscribed on it. It was our family seal. I read the words out loud. "Power. Protection. Loyalty. Forever."

There were tears in Mom's eyes. She brought my head to her breast. "My child. You are a baby no more. And I will never call you baby again. My body releases you. My baby is dead."

She gently pushed me away then and let out a long whooping wail, which was soon echoed by my sisters. Their wails were the primal female howls of mourning, and evoked the sadness felt by women when the youngest child dies. These emotions overcame me and I wailed, too. My voice reverberated throughout the house.

Soon Cici and Aurora were crying hysterically as Mom babbled in an unrecognizable language. I heard others within the house respond; Dad, our male siblings, and the staff all stopped what they were doing, and soon other women throughout the house were wailing without knowing why. The walls began to vibrate with the despair in my voice. I had to stop. I withdrew the sound waves, sucked them back into me gradually until the room, the women, and the house returned to a normal vibration.

Mom exhaled long and hard, and we all followed her lead. Our dresses were spotted with red tears. "It is good," Mom said. I noticed the drops on my own dress. She waved a finger and the red lifted out of the fabric. "No blood on you. Not yet."

"It's time," Cici said.

The family congregated in the great room. Dad and my brothers wore traditional, white Egyptian-Nubian kilts that stopped just above the knee. Even the twins wore white. Bare-chested, they all wore skullcaps, from which hung the eye of Horus in the middle of the forehead, similar to the skullcaps worn by Mom and my sisters. They wore heavier gold necklaces featuring our family seal. We all had the red armlets and small daggers. A small alter draped in white bore a gold bowl, a single white candle, and fresh white flowers.

Mom led me to Dad, who took my hands in his. We stood facing each other before the Yah, which now also bore our family seal. There was no one else in the house but us. I could hear the musical hum of Dad's wall of protection surrounding the entire property. We were all together as a family for the first time in my existence.

Dad was very calm, but his baby had died, too. My eyes welled up again. "My dear," he said, "you are embarking on the road of forever. Know that your family is your life. Know that we are one. We are bound together for eternity."

He faced the Yah and extended his hand to it. He spoke the ancient Nubian words inscribed on our seal. "Power. Protection. Loyalty. Forever."

My brothers extended their hands toward the Yah and repeated the chant. They then formed a circle around me and in a mighty voice chanted, "As one!" with their fists together over my head.

Dad stayed in his spot, hand extended to the Yah. Mom and my sisters entered the circle and joined my brothers. Reaching their hands over my head, they spoke the Nubian words together. "Power. Protection. Loyalty. Forever." They stepped back and formed a circle around my brothers and me.

"Daughter of light, drinker of life," Mom said in English. "We welcome you."

"This house is protected," Dad said, also in English. "This family is the law. And so it is." His magic was so thick the air vibrated in the key of E. "Aamiyn," he exclaimed in Aramaic. An ice-blue stream of energy shot from his hand into the Yah, which ignited as if on blue fire and began to glow steadily.

"Aamiyn!" we all repeated.

Dad pulled his knife and cut his wrist. He let the blood flow into the bowl. Mom followed suit, and then my siblings, in order of age. I was the last. When I was done, the bowl was passed around in the same order. Everybody sipped and then the rest was used to anoint my forehead and the Yah.

Then it was over, and I was literally flying back up the stairs with Cici. As we made our way back into the closet, the sounds of staff filled the house again and the band started a sound check. Cici led me to the dressing room dais. "Stand on this," she said. She then pointed to a forest green brocade gown, richly embroidered and shot through with gold thread. "Your receiving gown. One of the most important pieces of clothing for the Mahá."

A knock at the door revealed Mandarin Woman with her team. "We have her," she said to Cici. "The rest of your family is ready."

Cici turned toward the door. *Wait!* I yelled in my head. It was all happening too fast. She hesitated at the door, casual enough so no one would realize we were having a telepathic conversation. *I just wanted to say I love you. I'm so glad you're my sister.*

Her smile was brilliant as she turned to face me. *I'll never call you Bighead again.* "I'll see you soon, little sister," she said out loud.

And with that the style team commenced to rapidly dress, makeup, and hair me until I didn't recognize myself.

22. BE MY GUESTS

I sat on a throne in the receiving hall, a large multifunctional room off the waiting area. My gown, traditional and royal, was breathtaking, and my hair was done in a complex up-do and topped by a delicate gold crown. I felt as stiff as a board.

Guests filed neatly into a formal procession as they greeted me from a line that seemed to stretch forever. Many were familiar faces I recognized from Cici's Mahá pics, and many were total strangers.

My grandparents were the first, as was their right. Looking like they were in their early 30s, they dumped a small mountain of presents at my feet before moving on. Then came aunts, uncles, cousins, and more cousins. Cici's boyfriend Satchel flashed me a friendly grin, then proceeded down the line. But no one leaned in to hug me or shake my hand.

It's forbidden for anyone outside the immediate family to touch a newborn before the ceremonies commence. Cici explained. *That way no one gets hurt, or into anything unexpected.*

I remembered the way I snarled at her when I'd first woken up and felt my face burn with shame.

Don't worry about it. You should have been there when I woke up.

She placed that memory, from her point of view, in my mind: she was flying over Beacon Hill, while below Dad frantically cast invisibility spells to keep her from being seen and Mom set up force fields to keep her from going too far. I stifled a laugh.

A guy with long hair that rose on his head in a cone-shaped afro stood before me. He wore trendy gear, like he'd just stepped out of a music video. In fact, the last time I saw him, he was in a video. He was Little Wolf, one of the most popular rappers on the charts. He grinned wickedly before bending to kiss my hand and dropping it quickly, putting his hands up in a posture of surrender as my brothers instantly surrounded him. The guests pretended they weren't staring, even as the line grinded to a halt.

"What do you think you're doing, Markus?" Mom's voice rang like a death knell.

"I mean no disrespect, Mrs. Brown," Little Wolf/Markus said with sincerity. "It's been a long time since I saw Angel. That was the most special gift I could give her at the moment."

Mom's glowing eyes looked like she was going to continue her admonishment, but Dad put a hand on her arm. "Keep it moving," he said and gestured to my brothers to relax.

"Yes, sir." Little Wolf/Markus winked at me as he followed Dad's order, and bowed to the rest of my family before disappearing into the growing crowd.

You guys used to play together when you were kids. He had his Mahá three years ago. Cici placed an image in my mind of the nerdy kid he used to be when he'd spent summers with us before we lost contact with his family. Remembering how much fun we used to have playing together, I couldn't believe he was the same too-hip-for-the-room rap idol who'd just had the courage to kiss my hand.

After a few hours, I started getting bored with the parade of well-dressed immortals, and my mind started to wander. *Where are all these people going to sleep?*

Not all guests sleep over. Cici's face was expressionless. *Many choose to stay in nearby hotels, some teleport, or what have you. Mahá law dictates we attend the rituals and ceremonies. What we do in between is our choice.*

Finally, the procession ended and Mom and Dad stood up to address the crowd. "Welcome to the Mahá of Isis Angelica Clarissa Brown Ami-seshet," Mom said.

"We welcome you to our home. You honor us with your presence," Dad said.

As one, the crowd responded, "We welcome your authority and you honor us with your trust."

The band broke out with a Frank Sinatra number and people started mingling. Folks hugged each other as if they hadn't seen each other in centuries (as was likely the case with some of them), while many stood off to the sides to observe. Waiters walked around with trays laden with every edible, or potable, substance known to immortals, from mini-pizzas, to blood, to raw meat, to beer, to plants.

Cici whisked me up the stairs again. "Good grief, girl," I exclaimed. "Don't tell me I have to change again?"

"You have to change again. Now that you've seen what your guests are wearing, choose something as different as possible. You'll be mingling with the visitors so it shouldn't be too formal."

"Just shoot me now and get it over with. Oh, wait a minute, I can't die." I sighed in resignation. After all, picking out attractive outfits wasn't so bad. It was just the Mahá. I was already sick of it and it was nowhere near done. "How many more rituals and ceremonies are there, Cici?"

"There's the Abilities Showcase, then the Character Gauge. And last, the Vampiric Reaction Test. Not necessarily in that order."

"Vampiric Reaction Test? What on earth is that?" She eyed me. "Okay, I get it, you don't really know until you're in it."

"All I can tell you is these ceremonies are old as the Mahá, but they've developed over time. They give insight into not only who you are, but what you are capable of. There will be times when you learn a thing or two about yourself. If anything, we'll see for sure just how 'different' you are."

I picked out a pair of deep purple leather pants and a tangerine-colored blouse. The pants flared out like bell-bottoms. Green, snakeskin, pointy-toed, stiletto-heeled boots completed the bohemian look. "Is that 'different' enough?" I asked.

"I would have never thought the boots would work, but they do," she said in approval as I completed the look with gold filigree and semi-precious stone accessories. "Mingle," she said before pushing me out the door.

Unsure what to do, I walked woodenly to the crowded great room. Various people met my eyes, nodding politely. Everyone seemed so stiff. I figured I should engross myself in some sort of meaningful conversation. What did one talk about during one's own Mahá? "Hi, I just learned how to control my killer voice, but still can't stop freezing time. Have a nice day."

As I watched the band play a Duke Ellington tune, an idea began to bloom in my mind. Just then, Markus walked

161

toward me with a glass in his hand. "You have nothing to drink. I can get you some blood," he offered.

"No thanks, I'm good."

"You enjoying all this?"

"Not, yet," I answered as I grabbed his hand and pulled him onto the stage. I asked the band to play an old-school R&B jam and started doing the only thing I felt comfortable doing—singing. I practiced Mr. C.'s "note infusion" method by funneling my desire for some liveliness into my voice, but was careful not to lose myself like I did the night at the Garden. Folks gathered around the stage and started dancing, clapping, and smiling. Ah, that was so much better.

Markus bobbed his head to the smooth beat and flashed a toothy grin. His canine teeth were unusually pointy. There was no mistaking what he was now that he was all grown up. Not to mention that his stage name was kind of a give-away. He started freestyling an old-school, romantic rap. A number of the ladies in the room cheered in appreciation.

"Now I'm beginning to enjoy my Mahá," I said as we jumped down from the small stage to applause.

"Maybe we can collaborate someday."

"I'll have to talk to my partners," I answered, remembering what happened the last time I did my own thing without including the rest of Kat Trio. "See what they think."

There was a comfortable pause while we listened to the sounds of various activities around the house. There was a karaoke session happening in the north wing, a volleyball match starting in the sandpit, and a poker game going on in the mini-casino. Suddenly, it sounded like a fight was breaking out very close to us. "Hypocrite!" someone a few feet away yelled. We looked over to see Uncle Set who, as I remembered, was always angry. From his scowl and confrontational tone, nothing had changed. His body had gone rigid and the air around him started to crackle. I also remembered that he was a shape-shifter capable of changing into anything, real or imagined.

This was bad.

"Not in our house!" Mom's roar reverberated through the molecules of the air. She pointed to the Yah. It was glowing red, like her eyes. She looked frightening, but even scarier to me was Dad. His easygoing demeanor was replaced by a martial stance and his eyes were ice blue. His rarely-used wand, ancient with mysterious engravings, was unsheathed and in his left hand. My brothers and sisters had every exit covered.

Oh no. It seemed as if my Mahá would be *that* Mahá: the one where something really, really, reaaalllly bad happened. Anxiety started kicking in.

Set fell to his knees in front of me. "Please accept my apologies. I have dishonored your house, your authority, and your trust."

And then it came. The moment after which nothing would ever be remotely safe again. Uncle Set started to writhe in pain. Around the room, mortals fainted while immortals sank to the ground, some gasping for breath, some even screaming. Mom was panting. Dad walked toward her as if he was trudging through a vat of molasses. But I felt okay. Was this another power I didn't know I had?

But it wasn't me this time.

"They're coming," Mom gasped. Murmurs of fear rippled through the room.

"They?" I asked. Who were "they" and what did they have to do with what was going on?

Cici lay immobile on the floor, but her brain worked. The signal was very weak, but I could still hear her. *The Ancient Ones. They're coming.*

23. ANCIENT ONES

As soon as Cici told me the Ancient Ones were coming, there was a deafening ripping noise.

They travel between dimensions.

Suddenly there were two people standing in our midst. A woman and what may have been a man. The woman looked young, but her demeanor was of someone who was old enough to make Mom seem like an infant. And that was where all the Ancient One-ness came to an end.

I had pictured AOs in flowing, Biblical-type gear, like Menelik and Memnon, but she wore a pair of skinny jeans and black Mano Blanik heels. A gold and platinum Rolex with diamonds peeked out from underneath a crisp, tailored shirt and avocado-colored blazer. Her companion was over seven feet tall and androgynous. S/he wore a black leather trench coat and never met anyone's eyes. Looking at her/him made my stomach feel itchy, in a queasy way.

Dad and Mom made it across the room to stand by my side. Aurora and my brothers were still stationed around the room. Cici was leaning on a wall, and Markus was in the corner regaining consciousness. *Age*, Cici transmitted. *The younger you are, the less strength you have in their presence. Some even lose their abilities temporarily.*

Then why am I still standing? I asked. *Why do I feel the same as I did before they came?*

Our eyes met. I could hear her, but she couldn't hear me. I suddenly felt completely alone, but thank goodness, Mom and Dad each put a protective arm around me. We faced our newest guests.

"Welcome to the Mahá of Isis Angelica Clarissa Brown Ami-seshet," Mom said measuredly.

"We welcome you to our home. You honor us with your presence," Dad said in the same tone.

The woman inclined her head slightly in acknowledgment before pinning me with her gaze. How rude. This was, after all, my house. Why not show respect to my parents?

"Who are you, please?" I asked. "What is your name?"

There was a collective gasp from the others in the room. Even Mom and Dad stiffened. The woman's soft laugh sent chills down my spine.

"You may call me Cassandra."

"Thank you for coming." I said, conscious of addressing a being that just *looked* human. I nodded toward Trench Coat to include her/him in the welcome.

Cassandra leveled a look at Set, who was still on his knees. He literally shook. Pointing to Set, she said, "We want to see the Character Gauge now."

Mom clapped her hands and people sprung into action. What was happening? I looked at Cici as subtly as I could, hoping she could give me a clue. She was one step ahead of me, struggling to think as loudly as she could. *Relax and be*

*yourself. We all have the greatest faith in you and know
you'll do well.*

That was it? I had no idea what to expect or do.
Obviously, thinking on my feet was to be a part of these
rituals.

Dad turned to me. "Angelica. Set disrespected the
authority of this house embodied in the sacred Yah. How
should he be punished?"

Was this a test of my knowledge of Mahá tradition?
"As far as I understand, that sort of behavior is punishable
by death." Everyone hung on my words, and it struck me
that whatever justice I verbalized would be executed.

Set, eyes cast down, didn't seem angry anymore, just
scared. I felt sorry for him, but knew that if he wasn't dealt
with properly my family would appear weak. I was almost
one hundred percent sure that were it up to my parents he
would have been destroyed by now. His fate was literally in
my hands.

I thought about how he seemed to be angry and
negative all the time. It was almost as if he was broken.
Without further hesitation, I opened my mouth and directed
an A note straight at the space between his eyes. If he was
broken, I would try to fix him. The sound waves sunk into
his forehead and he started to cry. Then he spoke in a weird
language. I stopped singing when he fell, laughing, to the
ground. The sound of his laughter was almost as shocking
as the sight of the smile on his face (if you could call his
crazy leer a smile). The stunned gasps from the guests who
knew Set confirmed my observations. Getting the attention
of immortals who'd seen and done it all wasn't easy, but it
looked like I'd accomplished that with my brand of justice.

Another ripping noise, and a third AO was in our
midst. Under a uniquely embroidered gold cape, she wore
shapeless blue jeans and nondescript casual wear. Her
tangled blond hair hung wildly about her shoulders and,

although she looked about five-foot-two, she held herself as if she could dropkick the world.

"Moira," Cassandra said to the newcomer. "Did you see?"

"I saw," Moira replied.

Mom and Dad stood stiff as steel while addressing Moira with the perfunctory greeting. She barely looked at them as she trained her eyes on me.

I kept my gaze on Moira steady while thanking my lucky stars I no longer had to use the toilet in the same way since becoming immortal. If I did I would have peed my pants by now. She took a step toward me. For the first time I saw Trench Coat stir as s/he put her/his hand to her/his hip.

"We are here to observe. Nothing more," Cassandra said to Moira.

"You dare tell me what to do?"

"I dare."

From underneath her cape, Moira drew a sword and pointed it at Cassandra.

Trench Coat drew out a sawed-off shotgun from under his/her coat and pointed it at Moira. The human immortals let out a collective gasp. Murmured phrases of shock in different languages met my ears. I felt like I was having a heart attack.

Then the freezing thing happened again and the only ones capable of moving were me, Cassandra, Trench Coat, and the lovely (not) Moira, who now pointed her sword at me. "Die!!" she screamed wildly.

A third ripping noise brought the escalating situation to a halt when two more AOs arrived. At least I thought they were AOs. One was hooded, face hidden within depths of voluminous white linen. The other one looked like a tall six-year-old with wide, liquid eyes and a soft jawline. He wore white jeans, a white linen shirt, and white boots. His skin was jet black and his short, wavy hair was white. He looked so innocent I expected to see wings.

Both Moira and Cassandra backed away from them. Moira dropped her sword and Trench Coat handily returned the gun back to underneath her/his (its?) coat. I was too tongue-tied to ask the new arrivals their names.

"My name is Bodiel," the man said to me. His deep voice reverberated in my ears, and in my head, like the sound of the ocean in a seashell. The robed figure took off her hood to reveal her face. "My companion, Knowledge." She was the exact opposite of him: pale white skin with jet-black hair.

Cassandra and Moira both dropped to their knees. Trench Coat remained standing. This was just getting weirder and weirder.

"Excuse me," I croaked before clearing my throat. "But it seems as if I am the only one able to welcome you. Thank you for coming to my Mahá. You honor me, I mean, us with your presence."

Bodiel and Knowledge both regarded me with surprised expressions before bowing their heads and saying in unison, "We welcome your authority and you honor us with your trust." Their piercing gazes took in all the frozen immortals within the room. I looked around the room, too, mortified.

"Do you know why this happens to me?" I asked them. "How do I control this?"

"This is why she must be destroyed," Moira said from where she was still kneeling on the floor. "If she doesn't know what she's capable of, with power of this magnitude what can we expect? She may be the Dark One's twin flame. Or worse."

She could only be talking about Tunde. I didn't know what kind of chaos my brother had caused, but I did know the destruction of other immortals was a grave offense. If my own family was concerned I might be a Tunde repeat, it was no surprise these beings might think so, too.

"I am not my brother," I declared in a voice as firm as I could muster under the circumstances.

"This same thing happened at the large human event called a concert," Cassandra said as if I hadn't spoken. "She sang, and everything and everyone stopped."

Not everyone, but this didn't seem to be a good time to mention I had a reflection who had taken on a life of her own. Perhaps I would die today after all.

"You will not die today," Bodiel said. He was reading my thoughts as they popped into my head. "You have a twin flame. But it is not the Dark One. And as for your reflection..." He looked pointedly at Cassandra. We all followed his gaze, and after a few seconds, Cassandra morphed into the Lady.

For a second, I was flabbergasted. And then in a flash, I was standing in front of her, nose to nose. "How dare you come here after what you did to me and my family?"

With a casual flick of her hand she lifted me off the floor and I was suddenly hurtling through the air, on a collision course with one of the floor-to-ceiling picture windows through which I could see the huge, orange-tinged full moon in the distance. I braced myself and went through the glass without breaking it.

Once outside, I briefly marveled at the beauty of the clear, inky sky and brilliant stars, before realizing I didn't know how to stop hurtling through the air. Darn that Cassandra, or whatever her name was. A flurry of wings suddenly surrounded me. It was Bodiel and Knowledge. She grabbed me and brought me gently down to land on the ground.

"You have wings!" I exclaimed.

"We are not what you refer to as Ancient Ones," Bodiel said. He was still in the air, white wings fully extended into a fluffy nine-foot span. They undulated gracefully as he floated above our heads.

"You're such a show-off," Knowledge said, looking up at him with a loving expression on her glowing face. "Angel, we are what humanity calls archangels."

I exhaled wildly. I was meeting my namesake. They weren't what I expected angels to look like. But then again, nothing in my new life seemed to be what I expected, I thought giddily. My train of thought was nothing sort of mental babbling, but hey, one didn't meet angels everyday.

Bodiel touched down as Knowledge continued. "Unlike your ancestors, the Ancient Ones, we always stayed aligned with our purpose, so yes, we have wings. But wings are just a symbol of our completeness. Your Ancient Ones lost their wings a long time ago. It simply means a part of them is gone."

"But some of them are trying to make up for it," I said. "Atone—"

"We do not judge," Bodiel gently interrupted. "It is not our place."

If they were not here to judge me, then why were they here?

"We're here to help you, Angel," Bodiel said.

A mental image of the frozen Mahá popped into my mind. "We will show you how to control this," Knowledge said. "We will stay for the rest of your Mahá."

"If there is room for us, of course," they added in unison.

I had no clue whether there were extra rooms or not, but I wasn't about to turn them away. They were angels, for crying out loud! "Yes, you can stay as long as you'd like to."

Knowledge made a gesture and Moira and Cassandra appeared.

"We will stay here at this Mahá," Bodiel told them. "Like we did the other one."

"And, like the other one, I will stay to prove you wrong," Moira said. She looked at me expectantly. Was this some arrogant way of asking me for a room?

Bodiel smiled. "Yes, she is extremely arrogant. That's why she fell."

"Bo," Knowledge admonished in a sweet tone, "It's kind of rude to continually read the humans' minds. Let her speak what she wants to share."

I wasn't about to say no to an AO, either, no matter how obnoxious Moira was. "Yes, you may stay here." I turned to Cassandra and Trench Coat, hesitating for a fraction of a moment before saying, "And you both, too." I suddenly felt very weak.

"The baby needs rest and food," Bodiel said.

"I am not a baby!"

"She has a temper," Cassandra tattled. "It gets worse when she's hungry."

I opened my mouth and directed a D note at her solar plexus. She fell away from me, cringing. Good.

"Don't ever pull your shenanigans with me again," I said through clamped teeth. The air shone a slight red around us. Trench Coat was suddenly in front of me. The shotgun was aimed at my nose this time.

I looked down the pitch-black barrel and my stomach flip-flopped. This was no ordinary shotgun. Inside the barrel was the red, barren landscape I had seen in my death vision during The Change. In the few seconds I looked down the barrel, the staggering desolation of that place burdened every part of my being. The small amount of energy I *did* have vanished and I felt completely drained.

"I enforce the law," s/he said, unfurling wings almost as large as Bodiel's. At first, I thought the wings were red feathers. But no, they were flames.

Bodiel shrugged as if this was all normal. "Angel. This is Shoftiel. Please don't take it personally. He's just doing his job."

Cassandra gave me that bone-chilling smile. "We're all just fulfilling our roles. Aren't we?" AO or not, she was truly annoying. But there was nothing I could do about her now besides ignore her as much as possible and try to wrap my head around this bizarre situation.

I surveyed them carefully. Knowledge glanced at Bodiel in a way that reminded me of my secret telepathic conversations with Cici. I almost slapped my forehead. Duh, of course they were telepathic, and were probably communicating right now. Meanwhile, Moira and Cassandra watched me like pit bulls. And then there was Shoftiel. Through the entire ordeal, he remained unmoving unless there was some threat of violence. Like a sentinel.

"Are you here with Cassandra?" I asked him while fighting to keep a quiver of fear out of my voice.

"I am here with no one," he answered without turning his gaze to me. "I am here to enforce the Law."

Then I understood. He was like the AO police. He just showed up with Cassandra, but he wasn't her companion like I had previously thought. He was an angel, too; an angel of justice. I remembered Mom's account of her Mahá, and how she'd said young Jesus was accompanied by AOs and others. Now I was sure those "others" were angels.

"We have come to help you, Angelica, but you will not tell anyone about us," said Knowledge. "No one in your family must know, or there will be consequences." She glanced significantly at Shoftiel.

"We will continue to work with you as long as you keep our identities to yourself," Bodiel added. "Your family will not be able to access your awareness of us, and, like other humans, will see only what we allow them to. Do you agree to this?"

"I don't like keeping secrets from my family," I answered. "It feels uncomfortable, as if I'm doing something wrong." I turned to Bodiel. "How do I know you're good? You may be evil and mean my family harm."

Moira caught me off-guard by breaking out in a gut-busting laugh. She laughed so hard she fell onto the ground and started hitting it with her balled up fists, leaving small holes in the grassy lawn.

"What're you laughing at?" I asked, ticked off. "You pointed a sword at me. And you," I gestured at Cassandra, "you masqueraded as my reflection. How do I know you have my best interests at heart?"

I looked at Shoftiel and shivered at the memory of what was in his gun. I then turned to Bodiel and Knowledge. "And you ask me to lie to my family. How can any of this be good?"

"She is right," Knowledge said. "There is good and bad amongst our ranks. This question is fair." She turned to me and soft white light cascaded from her skin, illuminating the area around her like a band of microscopic fireflies. "It's our job to help mankind," she stated. "But we also root out the bad stuff, so to speak. To reveal us would put many in danger. If we cannot count on your confidence, beings of all sorts—human, angelic and others—will suffer. This is all I can say about this matter. We ask you again. Do you agree to this?"

Bodiel moved closer to me. "What does your heart tell you, Angel?" His wings were tucked away, and his white hair glowed like a florescent halo. "Do you feel that we are bad?"

"No," I answered with a sigh. "I don't feel that way about you and Knowledge." I withheld my statements about the others. "But, if this is what you request, I will agree to it under one condition." Cassandra and Moira looked at me with surprise. Even Shoftiel started to look directly at me before catching himself. "As long as we have this agreement, you must promise not to listen to my thoughts unless I ask you to."

"We have a deal," Bodiel said.

"Now," Knowledge brushed the dirt off of her long white and gold dress, "let's get your Mahá back on track. First, you will need nourishment." She snapped her fingers and Justin appeared before me, laid out on the grass. He wore black flannel pajama bottoms, no top, and looked as if he'd been literally lifted out of his bed. They may have been archangels, but they didn't seem to get the knack of the social graces.

"Angel? Where am I?" Confused, he stared around at the others, and I could only imagine what his mortal eyes perceived before they rested on me. "You okay?" he asked.

"I'm fine, Justin, just really weak. You're in California. These are my... friends." I waved in their general direction. "They brought you here, because I'm extremely hungry." I touched his shoulder. "I need you."

"I'm here for you, Angel," he said, pulling me down onto the grass.

"Privacy," Bodiel said, and everyone was zapped away, leaving Justin and me alone. I was hungrier than I thought and eagerly began. After a short while, I felt like my old new self.

But something was wrong. Justin usually held me close after we were done, but tonight he didn't. In fact, he didn't do anything. And his heart wasn't beating anymore. I had drained him so quickly, he was already dead.

"Justin!" I shook him, trying in vain to reverse the damage I'd done. "Justin! No!"

Bodiel and Knowledge appeared at my side. "Do something, Bo," she told him. "This is our fault. She's only fed in a controlled environment. We allowed her to get too hungry to safely feed from one mortal."

"Bloodthirsty wretch," Moira muttered from hundreds of feet away.

Besides the anguish I felt for having caused it, Justin's death hit me as if a part of my solar plexus had been gouged out. It was actual physical pain. I floated in mindless despair as my hands reached out to him in vain.

"Your blood tie was very strong," Bodiel explained. "That is the distress you feel." He breathed into Justin's mouth.

"There is still a spark of life in him," said Knowledge. "He will live, Angel. But he will not...be the same."

Feeling a sense of relief, I was able to calm myself enough to touch down before her words sunk in. "What do you mean, he won't be the same...?"

Bodiel finished his angelic CPR and Justin sat up languidly, as if he were waking up from a nap. He stretched and rolled the muscles in his back as a faint glow emanated from his skin. He regarded me as if he was seeing me for the first time. He said only one word, "Angel," before folding me into his arms and kissing me.

The kiss was cool and slow. And safe. His breath was sweet, and held his dominant scent of jasmine. I couldn't stop my body from responding. Justin's lips grew hotter as he stroked my hair, eyebrows, cheeks, my chin... I finally pulled away in an attempt to come to my senses.

"Is this what you meant by him not being the same?" I asked, referring to the kiss.

"No, we had nothing to do with that," Knowledge answered as she watched him closely. "He's no longer mortal."

"What? No! He won't have a normal life anymore."

"Would you rather he were dead?"

Despite the shame I felt at being the reason why Justin's life was taking a complete one-eighty, I had to admit I needed him alive. The tie was too strong and the pain was too real. But was it right?

"It's okay, Angel," Justin said. He turned me to face him. "I want this. And I know you want it, too." His tone was intimate. Sensual. He nibbled my neck.

"I don't know what you're talking about," I said, liking the sensations but feeling confused.

"You don't have a boyfriend," he stated.

"Excuse me? That's none of your business," I retorted. I pushed him away. "I'm not getting emotionally involved. And I suggest you don't either."

I started to turn away from him, but he took my hand and kissed it almost reverently. It was just too much to take. First he was dead and now he was acting like my lover. Even worst than the guilt of killing him in the first place was the guilt of not feeling the same way he felt.

"You can't tell me how to feel, Angelica. You can't dictate to me what's in my heart. I will always love you."

"Justin, please don't."

"Angel, don't you see? It's only right that now I can have something in common with you. For you to see me as an equal. If I can continue to feed you, I will gladly do it for eternity."

Knowledge and Bodiel looked at each other with raised eyebrows.

"Thank you," Justin said to Bodiel. "You've given me something priceless. I can never repay you."

"You're welcome," they said in unison.

Between the still-frozen Mahá and my love-struck, immortal donor, I was completely overwhelmed. "I'll deal with you later," I said to Justin. "Go home now." He didn't move. "Please?"

"I don't know how," he said. "Maybe I can just stay here with you?"

I looked to Bodiel. "He should at least go back and put some closure on his relationships. What about his family?"

"You'll have to close chapters in your mortal life eventually," Knowledge said to Justin. "But you need not do any of that tonight. Go home and Angel will be in touch with you soon."

Bodiel zapped him away before he could protest. "It would seem," he said as he rubbed his hands together, "that although his flesh is now immortal, his emotions and mind continue to be mortal. Fascinating."

I shook my head, thinking of the implications of what just happened and what it meant for my relationship with Justin. But I couldn't dwell on it now, there was another four-alarm fire burning. "Can we get the Mahá back to normal?" I asked. "Why is this frozen-in-time thing happening? How do I control it?"

"It's quite simple, Angel," Bodiel replied. "You have acute anxiety disorder. Your abilities get heightened the more anxious you get, and the resulting display is like a barometer. The more emotional you feel, the more intense the reaction."

"You've already figured out how to get things out of the time freeze and back to where they were the moment before," Knowledge said. "Now, you'll have to learn how to control your reactions so the freeze doesn't happen unless you want it to."

"My family's been helping me to stay calm."

"And they've been doing an excellent job. There's no reason to duplicate their efforts. Except in this one instance. When you freeze time, it's an almost instantaneous reaction and there's no time for them to do damage control. By the time they have a chance to respond, it's too late. They can't help you. But we can."

It was almost as if Bodiel and Knowledge had answered my prayer for help! They exchanged a quick glance before continuing. "We'll stick to the methods you've been using," they said in unison. "We'll help you calm down before things get out of hand. We'll show you how to channel this power so that you'll be in total control of it."

"Let's go back now," Bodiel said. Before he finished the sentence, we were all back in the great room, surrounded by my frozen Mahá. Everyone resumed their positions: Moira with her sword, Shoftiel with his shottie, and Cassandra with her bared teeth.

I started re-circulating the molecules as I had done in the Garden. "Wait a minute." I stopped to face Knowledge, "How do I explain my now-immortal donor to Mom? Surely she'll see that he's changed?"

"Don't worry about it," she said. "I'll have it figured out by tomorrow. And we're just your typical Ancient One guests, okay?"

"Got it," I answered before continuing to stir the air. Soon the gasps were again coming from every human immortal except me. Knowledge and Bodiel were nowhere to be seen.

"Put that sword down," I bellowed at Moira. "And you," I said to Cassandra, "don't you come to my Mahá stirring up trouble." I pointed to the glowing Yah. "My family is still the law under this roof. You must honor our authority."

Dead silence from the guests, many of whom, I supposed, had never heard anyone talk like that to an AO before. Knowing they could say nothing that would go against the wishes of Bodiel and Knowledge, a mollified Moira sheathed her sword while Cassandra glared at me. Shoftiel, sure that Moira was no longer on the attack, put away his gun. Dad and Mom shot disapproving looks at me while Cici covered her open mouth with her hand. Nobody else moved. For one second, I wondered if they were frozen again. But, no. Everyone was just stunned.

I was too exhausted and hungry to care what everyone thought of my outburst. I motioned to the band to play something, and asked a shaking waiter to follow me with some pitchers of blood, before heading straight for my bed.

24. MAHÁ FROM HELL

"Idiot!" Cici said. "What are you thinking? Don't you know AOs can destroy you in an instant?"

Barely awake, I rolled over in the California king-sized bed to find my parents, brothers and sisters there in the room staring at me. I didn't know how to answer Cici's question without breaking my promise to Bodiel and Knowledge. I remembered the warning the angels gave me and the coolness with which Shoftiel pointed his otherworldly shotgun at my nose. I had to keep my family safe. The tightrope of secrecy I'd walked in the past paled in comparison to the one I was navigating now.

"Mom," I said. "You said there was a time when the AOs walked among us, even lived with us. Why should we be so afraid of them now?" Mom and Dad looked at each other.

"She speaks truth," Memnon said. It was the first time I heard him say a sentence in English.

"Angelica," Dad said sharply, "did the time freeze happen again?"

I sat up. Was I being paranoid, or were Adrian, Aurora, Menelik, and Memnon farther away from the bed than everybody else? "Yes," I answered carefully. "It happened again."

Keeping my mind locked, I casually glanced at Cici to see if she registered any awareness of the events that took place after the freeze started. Like Knowledge said, she had no idea. "I fixed it though," I continued. "I think I'll soon be able to control it completely." I left out the part about being tutored by archangels.

As if they shared one face, the twins threw me identical strange looks, and Aurora watched me with guarded eyes. I needed to work harder to convince them all I was okay. "Listen up, everybody. I am not Tunde. I am not about to go postal on Mom or anyone in this family—"

"Postal?" interrupted Memnon, confused. "What does this mean, this postal?" Menelik slid him an info-packed glance and Memnon immediately nodded in understanding. I continued.

"And I'm not going to go postal on anyone *outside* of the family, unless they try to harm one of us. Power, protection, loyalty, forever. Right? So please stop staring at me like I have an extra head growing out of the side of my neck." I looked each one of them in the eye, begging them silently to believe me. Eventually, even Aurora relented.

I zipped into the dressing room. Cici was already in there. "Wear what you want," she said. "You don't have the next ritual until this afternoon and 'til then everyone's free to do whatever they want." She peered at me for a moment. "There's something different about you, Angel. It seems like you grew up when we weren't looking. And even though we're locked, I don't know exactly how or when it happened."

I wanted to tell her what went down when she wasn't looking, but there was that tightrope again… She continued. "I know there's more. I'm not even sure why except for something Mom told me. She said there was a part of you that was hidden away. Inaccessible."

I remembered eavesdropping on Cici and Mom's conversation, but I never told her that the two-way thing had happened. Suddenly, it seemed like I was hiding everything from everybody and for a moment, I felt very shady.

I still have faith in you, she was saying in my head. *I know you're not another Tunde. Or worse than Tunde. Just be careful, sis.*

She left me to dress. Demeter came in, but I waved her away. I wasn't up for dealing with the groupie vibe right now. Looking relieved, she darted quickly from the room like a scared rabbit. Oh well, the Mahá madness cost me a fan.

When I emerged, the opened French doors to my patio revealed an elaborate spread of various blood types in heavy, cut-crystal goblets. A warm Pacific breeze fluttered the linen tablecloth as well as fresh flowers in an elegant vase.

I was hungry, but took a second to appreciate the view. The deep azure blue of the ocean formed a sharp line of contrast against the powder blue of the sky. I inhaled the tangy salt air, along with the scents of various animals, abundant plants, and freshly cut grass.

"Mind if I join you?" Justin said, leaping onto the patio from the ground about twenty-two feet below. He took off his winter jacket and threw it on the floor. It was still wet with whatever precipitation was falling in Boston.

"W—what?" I stuttered. "How did you get here?"

"I haven't figured that out yet," he mused. "All I know is I knew you were hungry. I could actually feel your need tugging at me in Boston." He smiled as he fell into the seat across the table from me. "Before I knew it, I was here. I just followed your scent."

Wow. "Justin, we've got a lot to discuss, but this isn't the place to do it. If my Mom sees you, she'll know you're different, and we can't reveal what happened last night. You're going to have to go back."

"You're still hungry, Angel." He paused as if measuring something in his chest. "I don't think I'm capable of leaving you in this condition."

"You mean to tell me you can't help coming to me whenever, wherever I'm hungry?"

"I think so."

"And you can't leave while I'm still hungry?"

"Sounds about right."

Seriously? How was I going to be able to hide him from Mom if he showed up every time I got hungry?

Just then I heard moans coming from guests throughout the mansion and grounds. I ran over to the south window to look down on the pool. Guests were collapsing on the deck while some fell into the water and sunk to the bottom. Good thing they couldn't drown. Then there was a ripping sound and I felt the approach of something massive, like a huge boulder of energy rolling toward us.

More AOs, Cici transmitted. *Meet us in the great room. Now.*

"Justin, can you wait here for me until I get back?"

"Yes, I think I can physically stay here as long as you're not too far away," he said as I raced into the dressing room to put on something more Mahá-like.

"By the way," he called from the bedroom, "Bodiel and Knowledge are coming."

"How do you know?"

"They made me. I know when they come." Made sense. I threw on my own makeup and put my hair up in a simple, somewhat tall, bun.

The family was already in the great room, along with Moira, Cassandra, and other guests. I joined Mom and Dad just as the doorbell rang. We looked at each other, perplexed. Maximillian, one of the oldest immortals on the PE staff, made his way painstakingly, and with as much dignity as he could muster, to the door to open it.

There on the doorstep stood Bodiel and Knowledge, dressed as if they were ready to spend the day on the golf course; polo tops, khaki shorts, white socks, and Ray Bans.

"Please come inside," Mom said, before she and Dad offered them the perfunctory greeting. They responded sincerely as if it were perfectly normal to come in through the front door.

Like photonegative images of each other, Bodiel and Knowledge trained their gazes on me. It was obvious to everyone that despite their mortal dress and the luggage they cheerfully rolled in, they were very powerful beings. Fear-filled looks were directed at me by some of the guests. "It's a pleasure to meet you Angelica," they said. "We look forward to seeing the Abilities showcase next, unless there are objections?"

The question was directed to Cassandra and Moira, who quickly shook their heads "no." Shoftiel was nowhere to be seen, probably somewhere cleaning out his crazy gun.

"Excellent," Knowledge said. "We will retire to our quarters now, until we are called."

Mom gestured to staff to take the newest guests to their rooms and they were led away. You could hear a pin drop. As they passed by, I noticed they had no scent. How strange. Were all angels scentless, I wondered? I couldn't remember if Shoftiel had one, but since he scared the wits out of me, it was understandable that I hadn't taken the time to explore that side of him. Cassandra and Moira had scents even though neither had a heartbeat. Perhaps they had a scent because they had fallen. Or...maybe, Bodiel and Knowledge were masking their scents the way Adrian did when he was invisible.

Speculation ran wild in whispered conversations once they left the room. Immortals have a way of whispering that is hard to hear by other immortals, unless they are telepathic. To the mortal ear, the whispering sounds like a nearly inaudible hiss. I wondered what the guests were saying about this latest installment in my Mahá from hell.

"They are shielded," whispered Mom as she led me by the arm to a smaller private room. Dad and Cici followed shortly and she closed the door behind them. Dad raised his hand and another door magically appeared in the opposite wall. He quickly shepherded us into the room, and once inside, the door quickly disappeared. The room was empty and devoid of windows. There were no corners or edges, no ceiling. It felt like we were inside an airless, soundproofed orb.

"It's an Aeonion loop," Dad explained. "An endless loop of energy contained within a magical parameter. No one can see where we are or hear what we say."

Mom turned to me. "We have other new guests who came while you were getting dressed. They sit on the Council with me. Apparently, some think that my judgment of your abilities may be compromised because you are my child."

"The Abilities showcase could be problematic for you," Dad added. "The time-freeze ability may be seen as unredeemable because you cannot control it."

"The Council members may suggest your destruction today," Mom said, looking at my hand. She held it in her own the way she used to do when I was little, comparing the length of my fingers to hers and slowly tracing the shape of my fingernails. For her sake, I concentrated on my breathing and refused to let anxiety get the best of me.

"We can't let this happen," Cici cried. She was more agitated than I'd ever seen in my whole life.

"If the vote for destruction prevails, I cannot stop it," Mom's voice remained even despite the blood tears streaking her cheeks. Numbly, I realized I was crying, too, when her thumb swabbed a tear from my face. "There is no repeal process. The execution would be immediate."

Despite the news and the pain it caused, my feet stayed on the ground. I thought of Sawyer and promised myself that if I did live to see him again, I'd find out why I was even thinking about him at a time like this.

"I can make us disappear." Dad's voice was steely. "Right now."

Mom's face was grave. "We'd run for eternity. We'd have to take everyone we love with us, or they'd use them to draw us out."

This could very well be the last time we would be together. Whatever I said now was vital because it could constitute the last memory they had of me forever. I marshaled my thoughts and found my words. "I will not run," I said steadily. "No one will suffer because of me."

I wasn't afraid to die. In light of the destruction I could possibly wreak, it might be in the best interests of the family. Cici burst into tears. We lingered within the Aeonion Loop as long as we could, but eventually, Dad led us out to the outer room and we dissipated one by one back into the rest of the house. As I made my way back to Justin, I resigned myself to my fate.

"You're gonna die."

I turned around to see Moira leaning casually against the banister of one of the minor staircases. Her hair looked as if she never combed it, and she wore the same thing as yesterday, just more wrinkled.

"You have no say in whether I do or not," I answered.

"Not yet," she hissed. "But I have dibs for your head when the word's handed down."

I held her gaze and proceeded to pointedly brush my left shoulder off with my right hand as if flicking dirt in her direction. "Good luck with that," I spat before turning on my heel and walking away.

As I moved up the stairs, my stomach growled. I felt a sense of peace at the thought of Justin's familiar scent and taste and the post-feeding comfort I could find in his arms. When I got to my room, however, he was with Bodiel and Knowledge. "Is there a way to help him so that he's not a slave to my hunger?" I asked them.

"We've adjusted that," Knowledge answered.

"I'll still know when you're hungry, there's no way to stop that."

"But now he will have a choice and will no longer be compelled," Bodiel added. "We have also tweaked him so that he will not read as an immortal. Now we need to help you control your ability."

It was just like an angel one-stop repair shop. I quickly informed them of the appearance of the Council elders. Justin, whose angel-induced immortality and blood-tie bond of secrecy, allowed him to be in on everything that had happened, turned pale. The angels stared alternately at the floor and the wall for a few wordless moments.

"We cannot intervene in the decisions of the Council," they finally said. "To do so would disrupt the flow of free will. However, we will do all in our power to help you right now. You must work with us. If you put all your energy into this effort, we will be successful."

"Let's begin," Knowledge said.

"Wait," Justin interjected. "She still needs to eat."

"Of course," said Bodiel as he gently took Knowledge by the elbow and evaporated.

It occurred to me that Justin would suffer from the same blood-tie distress if I were to die. As he offered his neck I fervently hoped Bodiel and Knowledge could fix that for him, too, if it came to that.

Mealtime was different now that there was no limit to how long Justin could go. I couldn't believe he was still alive, although he grew lethargic the longer I fed. A few minutes later, I had my fill. "You still eat food?" I asked.

"Kidding? I could eat a horse."

Bodiel and Knowledge reappeared. After a communicative glance from them, Justin turned around to leave the room. "I'm going to find some grub," he said, before closing the door behind him. Fortunately, it was normal for a newborn to have a donor at their Mahá, so no one would think twice when they saw him in the house. I was ready for what was coming but felt very nervous, too. I took a deep breath.

"You are anxious," said Knowledge, "but not enough to trigger the time freeze." She grabbed me and started tickling me. I screamed in shock, and fought against her without thinking. "Give it all your effort. Control your anger."

I heard her clearly, but it was so hard. Ever since I was small, I absolutely hated being tickled. It made me angry and uncomfortable and icky-feeling and—

"There it is," Bodiel said. He went to the window and beckoned me over. Knowledge released me and I looked outside. Sure enough all guests and living things were frozen in time.

"Apologies, Angel," she said, "but that was the fastest way to get you to that point organically."

It was impossible to remain upset in the face of such courtesy. "No problem. Now what?"

"I see a brief moment, the equivalent of one sixteenth of a second where you may be able to use your will to stop the freeze before it is initiated," Bodiel said.

"So how do I do that?"

"Locate that brief moment of time. It may be something you see, hear, or feel. Concentrate. Will it to stop at that time and you will save yourself and your family."

I nodded, although what he said made no sense whatsoever.

"Let's get things back to normal," Knowledge said.

I did. So quickly that I impressed myself. Before I could finish patting myself on the back, however, Knowledge sucker-punched me square in the nose. The bridge cracked and red rage flooded my vision.

"There," said Bodiel. "Concentrate, Angel. There it is!"

Instead of screaming in rage, I took a quick breath through my mouth and willed myself to find what he was referring to. And then I saw it. It was a barely noticeable impression before my eyes; almost like a small button. I'd seen it before but didn't think it had anything to do with freezing time.

"Too late," Bodiel said. "Everything's frozen again."

"Saw it this time," I muttered while wiping blood from my face. "It's been there in front of me all along. Just didn't make the connection."

Knowledge smiled sweetly. "Unfreeze, Angel."

I did. And then I held up my hands in a "time out" gesture. I wanted to see if I could do it on my own, without the abuse. *Sorry*, Bodiel said distinctly in my head. My throat started to constrict as if someone were strangling me. But neither angel had moved to touch me. I couldn't breathe, couldn't do the one thing that calmed me down enough in order to function. I felt myself lift off the ground.

Where was it? Where was the button? I spluttered and coughed as the pressure on my windpipe increased. My voice will be ruined! I thought wildly. I saw the button and willed it to be pressed. Sure enough, the convex part of it clicked into concave as if I had pressed it with my finger.

The strangulation ceased. I drew in a long ragged breath before falling onto the floor. Knowledge came to my side. Afraid of what she might do next, I cowered away from her.

"Relax," she said. "You did it. You stopped the freeze before it initiated." She helped me up and, leading me to the bed, made me lie down. Bodiel came with a cool cloth and held it against my face. It felt soothing. My broken nose had already mended itself.

"The time freeze kicks in when you lose yourself in emotions, Angel," she continued. "It's important for you to step outside of panic, pain, and confusion in order to control this ability without exception."

I nodded in understanding, and used the now-warm cloth to wipe away the remaining blood. My throat still felt a little raw.

"Do you forgive us, Angel?"

"Yes," I said without delay. "After all, this is what will save my life eventually...isn't it?" Bodiel and Knowledge smiled at each other.

Instantly, we were standing on a landscape, but it was nowhere I could identify. We were surrounded by fire as far as the eye could see. There was a deafening roar of flames, and beneath that was constant howling. Even the sky seemed to be on fire. But the fire had a life of its own because there were no objects to burn. The ground was the color of blood and the heat was unbearable.

I turned back to Bodiel and Knowledge, but before I could ask them where we were, they shoved me to the ground and flew away. I was too scared to scream, too scared to cry and what was worse, there was nowhere to run. I stayed on the ground where I fell, cringing from heat so hot it made me burn.

I was wrong about Bodiel and Knowledge. They *didn't* have my best interests at heart. I'd been fooled, and would pay for my stupidity by dying here in this hellish place, alone. I attempted to take in a long breath, but the air was so hot it burned my throat. The smell of my burning flesh filled my nostrils and I vowed that if I got a chance, angels, or not, I'd hunt them down and kill them.

Then I heard the click. It was so familiar, I would have continued to ignore it if it hadn't just occurred to me. Suddenly, I made the connection. The clicking sound started the process of the time freeze. If I stopped the click, the freeze could not commence. Concentrating, I reversed the click so I wouldn't even get to the part of having to press the button. I controlled the time freeze completely by deciding when and where the click would or wouldn't take place.

I was immediately surrounded by a flurry of wings, and found myself once again back in my room. I was still on my knees in the same position I had been cringing in. Knowledge picked me up and gently placed me on my bed.

"That was all part of the test?" I managed to ask. My throat was scorched to the point where it hurt to talk.

"There's no need to talk, but only if it's okay with you," Bodiel said.

It's fine to talk this way, I transmitted. *Will my voice be okay?*

Knowledge stroked my hair while I watched light particles drift with their own awareness from the pores of her skin. *Rest and rejuvenate and all will be well.*

Would you really have hunted us down? The question caused a wrinkle to appear in Bodiel's inhumanely smooth face.

I was pretty mad, but I guess that was part of the test, too, huh?

No, Angel, he said. *The anger was all you.*

We laughed out loud, even though my laugh was weak and pathetic.

Did I make it?

Yes, I heard them both simultaneously. *We are confident you will be able to control the time freeze, and more importantly, control yourself.*

Rest. We will send Justin. Knowledge smiled. *We will not call for the ceremony until you've had enough time to rest.*

And then they were gone. Still on my back, I painstakingly pivoted my head to the left and ended up face-to-face with Justin laying next to me on the bed. "We really have to stop meeting like this," he joked. His laughing came to a halt as he took a closer look at me and his mouth turned into a grim line. "My god, Angel, what did they do to you?" He bit his wrist so that it bled and held it to my mouth. It was all I could do to open my lips and allow the blood to trickle between them. I drank this way for a few minutes until I fell asleep.

I awoke to a darkened room and growling stomach. Justin was still there at my side. "I told your folks you were exhausted," he explained. His voice sounded deep and soothing in the darkness. "They think it's from the news of the Council. And the Council thinks it's a reaction to the presence of the AOs." He placed his wrist to my lips again. "Don't worry, I've eaten a ton of food."

I drank more in stages. I was eventually able to hold up my head, then sit up, then push him back on the pillows and take my fill. It really was a good thing he was immortal now because I surely would have killed him a hundred times over with my insatiable need.

Soon, I was back to normal and drifting in and out of sleep. We lay still for a long time, listening to our hearts beat. His eyes were closed, but I could tell he wasn't sleeping. "Justin, what're you thinking of?"

"I don't want to be a cadet anymore. I just joined because it was expected."

His Dad, grandfather, three uncles and older sister had all been, or were, members of the Boston Police Department. "The oldest police force in the country," he continued. "You can't imagine the pressure to fit into an age-old family tradition."

"You'd be surprised at how much I can relate to that," I said wryly.

"Don't worry, Angel. I'll find something worthwhile to occupy myself with. I'm eighteen and just discovering now what I'd like to do with my own life. It's been a big transition, getting used to this immortal thing. There are things I can do now that I never dreamed of."

I could relate to that, too. He rolled over to his side to look at me while propped on one elbow, his face resting on his fist. "You mind if I just hang out here for the rest of your Mahá? It's the only place where I feel right."

I was amazed at how much Justin and I had in common. But why, when things were going wrong, was it Sawyer, not Justin, who popped into my head? Shouldn't it be Justin? After all, he was what you would call the total package—handsome, protective, sincere, and loyal. But Sawyer was taciturn, brooding, tense...and gifted, mysterious, and beautiful. And mortal. The implications of Justin's eternal devotion bounced around in my brain until I fell back asleep in his arms.

The next day, I felt like my old newborn self. Coiffed and dressed in a classy turquoise cocktail shift with sparkly silver heels, I, along with Cici, met the rest of the family in the Sound Room. Huge in width and height, and containing a small stage surrounded by hundreds of seats, it was more like an auditorium.

"The acoustics in here will allow people to handle the sound of your voice," Mom said as she led us inside. We sat down in a reserved section of seats, and soon guests started filing in. There was an air of eagerness and excitement.

Your voice is the star attraction, Cici transmitted.

Moira, Cassandra, and Shoftiel sat in another reserved section and were joined by Bodiel and Knowledge, who, this time looked as if they were dressed for a day on the yacht. Cassandra, openly eye-balling me, was lucky Shoftiel was close by or I would have torn her head off. Moira patted her sword dramatically and pointed at me. Whatever. After what the angels had put me through, I felt I could take anything she had for me.

There they are. The Council members.

It was Charleston and the other two council members from the night at the Garden. I transmitted that little bit of info to Cici. Stone-faced, I heard her telepathically relay the information to Dad, who whispered very quickly to Mom. Her eyes narrowed as if she were ready to do battle. Despite the angelic tutelage, my stomach tightened a little in anxiety. What if I failed the test and turned out to be a screw-up after all? I took a long deep breath.

In a few minutes, the room became packed. All seats were filled and the remaining guests stood shoulder-to-shoulder along the walls. Some people even claimed vertical space by floating way above the heads of the rest.

Mom quickly squeezed my hand before making her way to the front of the room. "As requested by our guests," she inclined her head toward Bodiel and Knowledge, "we will have the Abilities showcase now. All abilities that are not visible will be explained completely. Isis Angelica Clarissa Brown Ami-seshet, step forward."

Funny how I could perform in front of tens of thousands of people and not feel anywhere near the stage fright I experienced now. That probably had something to do with the importance of this particular performance; if it wasn't a crowd pleaser, I'd be killed. I decided right there that if this was to be my last gig, I'd give them a show to remember. I straightened my shoulders, raised my chin, and strode confidently over to Mom before looking over the faces of the guests. Markus/Little Wolf, wearing a red eye patch and a lime-green afro pick planted in his hair, gave me a thumbs up.

Just do whatever Mom says. You'll be fine, sis.

Mom inclined her head to the angels and AOs, and finally her fellow council members, before leading me through individual demonstrations of my abilities: levitation and speed. After each demo, Dad, positioned at the side of the stage, sounded a gong. The easy stuff was out of the way. I took a deep breath.

Steady, sis.

"The next ability will have to be explained first," Mom said. "Angelica can freeze time."

Ah, there they were. The gasps. The Council members stood up, and Charleston spoke. "We have witnessed this ability," he said. "Everyone and everything around us was frozen at the newborn's public performance." These last two words were spoken with distaste. "We request a repeat of this so we can see if she is in complete control of this ability."

Oh, heck in a hand basket. I didn't know how to make it affect some people and not others. That had been Cassandra's doing. I glared at her with all the anger I could stuff into a glance. Then I heard Bodiel's voice.

She will interfere the same way she interfered that night. It is the fair thing to do. Please proceed.

Okay. Now, how could I get myself to that place where I could hear the click? I had to make myself angry. I concentrated on Cassandra. In no time I heard the click, and saw the button. I didn't press it, just calmly let it go. I looked around. Half the guests were frozen and half were not. The unfrozen ones looked around in astonishment, as if they were standing in a museum full of abnormal exhibits.

Satchel was one of the unfrozen guests. "Seriously?" was all he said.

The angels and AOs looked around, too. As Cassandra performed a discreet gesture with her finger, the unfrozen guests, including my family, became frozen and the others unfroze. Now it was their turn to stare around them in amazement. The Council members and Mom remained unaffected through the entire thing. I took a deep breath and unfroze everybody.

Utter. Silence.

The long silent spell, replete with unblinking stares, was finally broken by the sound of Dad's gong. He looked at me with pride. Cici's eyes brimmed with tears of joy and Mom stared Charleston down. The Council members were speechless.

Mom spoke triumphantly. "And the final ability. Voice."

There was the sound of hundreds of people simultaneously leaning forward in their seats. More people in the back floated up above our heads to get a better view. I cleared my throat, which was still slightly raspy from the heat endured earlier. After singing a few upbeat scales, I offered an a capella rendition of "Jeux Veux Vivre." The guests grew happy with the music. I finished the song and addressed the audience.

"I can heal with my voice. And I can kill with my voice. You have seen a healing." I gestured toward Set. "And I have already killed, too. A bear. When I was less than twenty-four hours old. I will not kill here."

The Council members stood in unison again. Were they attached at the hip or something? "We need to see the level of destruction you can cause with your voice so we will know what we are dealing with," Charleston said.

This wasn't good. I looked to Mom and Dad.

"I am entering an official protestation, brethren" Mom calmly told her Council peers. "The execution of your request will put our guests in danger."

"Your protestation is noted, Sister Council" said a Council member who hadn't spoken yet. He turned to the guests. "If anyone wishes to vacate the room or the property, do so now and we will relinquish you of further Mahá attendance obligation."

Two guests quickly exited. They represented a cluster clan of over nine hundred families in Asia, the Middle East, and Africa. Everyone else stayed put.

Charleston looked smug. "We will proceed."

"*I* protest," I said. There were murmurs among the audience. "You don't know what you're asking. I don't want to hurt anybody." I glanced at Cassandra, remembering how even she had cringed at the sound of my voice.

Charleston was immediately in my face. He had fangs and he bared them like a wild animal. "Child, we are the law. We hold your life by a string. Do as we say."

I decided I didn't like this guy. Anybody who'd put other people in danger to prove a point wasn't the kind of person I'd invite to dinner. I looked toward the angels and AOs. Shoftiel held up his hands as if to say he had nothing to do with it. Bodiel and Knowledge inclined their heads. "As you wish," I said to Charleston.

I directed my voice at the stage and split it in two. I changed the key to F and the rift in the stage corrected itself. Amidst a few shocked whispers, I then directed my voice at the windows. A shaft of turquoise-colored sound smashed into the glass, and caused them to shatter into thousands of pieces while guests ran, flew, and otherwise disappeared from the area to the safety of other parts of the room. Again, I altered the key and the shards swiftly merged together as if they'd never been broken.

More whispers, littered with a few exclamations.

I then directed my gaze at Charleston. The room became quiet, as if everyone were holding their breath. Fear registered in his eyes before I let loose a high G and aimed it directly at his heart area. *He asked for it.*

He fell to the floor screaming and thrashing around in pain.

"*Is that good enough for you?*"

I sang each word in the same note without stopping to take a breath, and held the note until he started smoking like a lit charcoal briquette.

"Yeeeessss!" he finally screeched in agony.

I immediately sent a healing B minor to wash over and soothe him. After a few seconds, he was able to stand, and eventually sit back down. Once he regained his composure, he nodded in frustration and resignation. I stopped singing.

Bravo, sis!

Uncle Set stood up and applauded. Justin visibly released a sigh of relief from his seat at the back of the room. Dad winked at me and banged the gong. And that was the end of the "hell" part of my Mahá from hell.

Or so I thought. At that moment everything stopped.

Oh, no! I looked around the room. Even the Council members were frozen. Bodiel and Knowledge stared at me. Cassandra and Moira walked toward me. I took one last look at my family before closing my eyes and praying the AOs would kill me swiftly.

25. STAR

As Moira and Cassandra moved closer, I wondered which one would murder me. "She's all yours," Moira said to Cassandra as if she heard my thought.

I opened my eyes. "This will be the last thing I do," I said to Cassandra before hurtling a high B note at her head. She narrowly escaped it by diving behind the stage.

"Stop," Knowledge said. I thought she was talking to me, but she was speaking to Shoftiel, who'd pointed his shotgun at me. His finger was on the trigger.

"Go ahead," I threw at him. "Shoot me with your hellified gun." I pointed to Cassandra. "She has to pay. She's done nothing but hurt me and my family."

"That's not true, Angel—" Cassandra inserted.

"LIAR!" I roared.

Cassandra cringed from the sound of my voice before extending her hand toward me. "I have protected you since the day you were born," she said softly. "I am Star."

And with that, the being I knew as Cassandra transformed yet again, this time into a light so bright it almost blinded my eyes. Soon, her brightness diminished as she took on the form she must have had eons ago when she decided to give it all up for love. Silenced by her almost painful beauty, I stood in shock as her face shifted. One second she looked like Mom, then she looked like Aurora, then Cici, me, and others I didn't recognize beyond a basic family resemblance. It was like looking at a multifaceted crystal and every facet was a part of me. Her loving gaze reduced me to tears. She truly was our mother. I fell to my knees in love, awe, and confusion.

"Why?" I pleaded. "Why be a reflection? Why all the subterfuge?"

"Like everyone else, I do not know if a newborn will be, as you say, good or bad. As your reflection I had an opportunity to get to know you over a longer period of time."

Her true voice sounded like musical bells. I was mesmerized.

"But all beings of this Earth have free will," she continued. "Therefore, I had to wait until you decided what type of person you would be before I revealed myself. I could not help or influence you. To do so would be deemed unfair. All I could do was protect you."

"But you fought me. You set me up at the Garden gig as if you were my enemy."

"Everything I did was to test you, and to give you the skills you will need to fight adversity. I called Bodiel and Knowledge when it was apparent you needed a little help with your ability."

"You called Shoftiel, too?"

She smiled that weird smile. "Don't you know by now, Angel? Earth-bound immortals cannot stop you. There was still a question as to what direction you would choose." She touched my face with fingers that felt like warm honey.

"If you'd given me a reason, I would've killed you in a heartbeat," Moira grumbled.

"But now it is clear to us who you are," Bodiel spoke. "We are satisfied."

"This ability you have, your voice," Star said. "You have used it well. And we are proud." Her maternal tone reminded me of Mom. I felt her lips on my forehead before everything unfroze and went back to normal. And then she was gone, along with Moira and Shoftiel. With no idea of what just took place, the crowd dispersed.

Soon after, Bodiel and Knowledge made their way to the front door with suitcases in tow. Knowledge turned to me. "Well done, young one." She actually hugged me. Bodiel patted me on the back, much like one would pat a dog considered to be a treasured family member.

"What about Justin?" I asked. "How will I explain what's happened to him?"

Bodiel smiled. "You'll work it out."

Mom, Dad and Cici came to my side. "Thank you for honoring us," Mom said. The angels bowed their heads humbly and started to turn away.

But I just had to ask. "What's in the suitcases?"

"You really want to know, Angel?" I nodded eagerly. "Souls," they whispered together, before the door closed with a final, loud click.

I let loose a wild exhale before Cici turned to me. "You did it!" she exclaimed with tears and a big smile.

Dad gave me a bear hug. For a brief moment, I enjoyed the pleasure of feeling protected, but I also relished the fact that my safety had been earned with my own pain, anxiety, and blood. "One more ritual to go," he said warmly, smiling down at me.

"It will be nothing," Mom added, wrapping her arms around us.

"Good," I said in relief, "Because this Mahá is killing me." We all laughed at my corny joke before Cici and I made our way back to the dressing room.

# # #

Fifteen minutes later, I was freshly showered and changed. The house's energy was back to human level, and now that the AOs were gone, folks were more relaxed. That is, until I came around. Then, they straightened up (as if they'd been talking about me) or moved out of my way. The euphoria I felt from having stayed alive melted away. My knees buckled and I sank onto a bench right before Justin appeared.

"You're hungry and tired," he said. He picked me up like I weighed two ounces. "It's been a long day."

His arms felt good around me. Familiar. Wanting to hide from the fear in my guests' eyes, I allowed myself to relax and melt into him. He started walking toward the nearby service stairs. "Where are we going?"

"To the bedroom," he answered as if it were obvious.

"Justin!" I exclaimed. I tried to get out of his arms, but his new strength made it difficult.

"Angel, it's not what you think. I mean, you need to eat." I stopped struggling, but still wanted him to let me go.

"Justin, you can't let my family see this. I still can't explain—"

"Explain what?" Mom said from one of the doorways off the hallway. "You are free to bring your donors to your Mahá."

Her eyes took in the ease with which he carried me.

"I've been working out," he said, trying to cover. "Eating lots of protein."

Her brows knitted and her fingers twitched. She wanted to touch Justin; to scan whatever she sensed was off. Despite all I'd been through, I was still afraid of being busted by Mom.

"Mom, I'm about to eat the mortal staff," I blurted, hoping that would bring her ruminations to an end. It did. She stepped aside to let Justin sweep me up the stairs, away from the guests.

Later, the family, and Justin, lounged in my suite while Cici helped me get dressed (yet again) in the dressing room. "All you need to do," she said, "is drink blood from a person. The Vampiric Reaction ritual is simply a gauge of what kind of blood drinker you are.

"What's the point?" I asked.

"When feeding from mortals, Shimshana occasionally create vampires accidentally," Mom said from the suite. "We are unsure why some mortals are affected this way, but our DNA is responsible for the existence of a number of vampiric striations, including the ones with fangs, the ones that sparkle in the sun, and the ones that cannot bear the sunlight. That, my dear, is how vampires came to be."

I thought about this for a second, and then it hit me: the ritual could be a perfect cover for Justin's new abilities. That was probably what Bodiel meant when he said I'd "work it out." Later, when Justin didn't drop dead after I'd fed from him past the limit, and he demonstrated his newfound strength, the Council members proclaimed him a vampire who could walk in the day and didn't have fangs.

"Just don't let anyone see you eat that," I warned him afterward, as he raided the buffet for an entire roasted chicken and a few sandwiches.

After the rituals were done, it was time for the public face of the Mahá. Many immortals took their leave at this

point, including Mom's Council colleagues, which was fine
by me. To celebrate, Markus and I did a couple of songs
from his first album as press photographers captured some
shots, thanks to PE sending out word through the
Hollywood grapevine. We wrapped up our impromptu
performance to thunderous applause. "They love us
already," he said right as the band blared a rousing salsa
intro. He started spinning me around the dance floor. "By
the way," he continued, "you were brilliant at the Abilities
Showcase. Come out sometime."

"You're asking me out on a date?" I asked in disbelief.

"May I cut in?" Justin interrupted. Markus emitted a
low snarl before reluctantly giving my hand to Justin.

"Haven't I shown I can take care of myself, Justin?" I
whispered angrily, resenting his possessive attitude.

His answer was to press my body into his as we
swayed together. "No one knows you better than me," he
said in a low voice. He was right. He was the only person
who knew about the angels. And he was the only one I
could tell about Star. He wore an Armani suit that
Wardrobe happened to have hanging around in their surplus
stock. His five o'clock shadow brought out the blueness of
his eyes. I had to admit; he looked good. The small army of
women checking him from the sidelines seemed to think so,
too.

"I once wondered if it were the blood obsession that
made me feel the way I do about you," he continued. "But
then I remembered the first time I laid eyes on you. I
walked to you, to be in your service, and had already fallen
under your spell." He held me even tighter. I felt every
angle, every crevice of him. "I wish you were hungry
now," he said longingly. "I really do."

"Justin, I think you need to find a girlfriend." I glanced
suggestively at one woman in particular who couldn't stop
staring at him. He followed my glance.

"As if I am so simple-minded that any girl would do?" he whispered angrily. "Angel, you're a goddess. Who can compare?"

I felt bad for suggesting he was easy. "Sorry," I stammered, "didn't mean it that way." We danced in silence for a few moments.

"When you go back into the mortal world," he said, "you'll see how much you've changed. You'll see it in the faces of everybody who you thought you knew. You'll see they don't know you at all."

He dipped me deeply as the music came to a climatic end. I felt his breath in my ear. "When you feel alone, call me," he whispered. "We don't need the waiter anymore. You don't even need a phone. All you have to do is feel me. And I'll be there for you."

26. LAYING IT DOWN

Justin's insight into my imminent alienation proved prophetic. I'd survived my Mahá, but back in Boston, the day-to-day reality set in.

I was a freak.

Instead of feeling like a card-carrying member of the immortal club, I felt like an outcast. Even some of my own family looked at me sideways. The twins avoided me, Adrian stopped sneaking up behind me, and Aurora and Roman were on pins and needles. Mortals were acting weird, too. Since the press came out on the Garden gig, kids at school who used to leave me alone now treated me like some sort of celebrity. Smiles were a little too big and enthusiasm seemed a little extra when I walked into a classroom. Even though it was months away, guys were asking me to the junior prom. People even let me cut the cafeteria line, though no one seemed to notice I never ate the food on my tray.

Thank goodness Jules and LaLa were the same. "Girl, we missed you!" LaLa exclaimed.

"You definitely seem more relaxed," Jules added. "You were looking mad stressed."

"I'm straight now," I said, knowing they could never understand how true that was. More than ever, I needed the everyday realness of my girls. I spent every waking moment with them: catching up, shopping with money we'd earned from the gig, and honing our vocals for the Sawyer tracks in prep for our upcoming recording session.

"He kept asking about you," LaLa confided. "He wanted to know if you were okay."

So he'd been thinking about me, too. Maybe what happened between us was real after all. The idea made my heart jump into my throat, and it took all I had not to pick up the phone. Jules looked at me with a knowing glance. "Our session's tomorrow," she reminded me. "You'll see him then."

Even though a mortal tomorrow was insignificant to me now, it still felt like forever before I'd see Sawyer again.

# # #

We entered Omega Blast, the professional studio where we were scheduled to record, as if we were walking into a sacred shine. Literally around the corner from Sawyer's studio, it was a place where many top acts had laid down tracks. We looked around in awe at the pictures and awards decorating the walls. Despite the demo CDs we put together in the past, the recording process was still relatively new to us. More than the adoration of the fans, I craved the respect of my peers, and the recording studio was the place where that respect was earned.

Nina had warned us the session could go all day before Sawyer felt like he had everything he needed, so I'd prepared myself by packing over twenty thermoses. I may have been in control of my voice and time-freezing ability, but when it came to being around Sawyer, I couldn't take any chances. Just the thought of seeing him again made me want to jump out of my skin.

We received a ton of spam from people who wanted to work with us, but the number of people we'd invited to record with us were few. We recruited Elio's bass player, Joy, and their drummer, along with the backup-band guitarist who had kept up with me so well the night of the Garden gig. The rest of the instruments, keyboards, percussion and such, were to be covered by Sawyer.

We also invited Markus to come over and drop eight bars. LaLa was ecstatic about this. She screamed when I asked her and Julietta if it would be okay to let him sit in on our session.

"What! Are you crazy? Little Wolf! Of course, it's okay with me!"

In a strange role reversal, Julietta was the more reserved one. "You never mentioned you knew him," she said in an accusing tone. "How'd you manage that?"

"Who cares?" LaLa said while bouncing around the studio. "Whoo hoo!"

I felt like I'd stepped into the Twilight Zone.

Sawyer, looking like he hadn't slept for days, introduced us to Don, the recording engineer. It was clear from the coffee cups, empty mineral water bottles, and various empty food packages strewn around that they had been at work for some time. They were now ready for us.

"Angel, you go first," Sawyer said from his seat at the boards. "I need your vocals laid down so I can build out the other vocal tracks around them."

Carrying my hot lemon-honey tea, I made my way into the main recording booth and put on the headphones.

"Sing into the mic, need levels." His grunted request emphasized the dark little cloud around his head and the deep frown above his red-rimmed eyes. In the soundproofed booth, I could smell the exhaustion coming off of his skin and it made me want to take away whatever was weighing on his mind. Complying with his request, I sang an F note. The sound of my voice fed back into my ears through the headphones as I placed my wishes into that note and directed it exactly where I wanted it to go. Straight to Sawyer's heart.

Sure enough, his frown became less deep, and I could see the space between his brows again. He was relaxing. "That's good, Angel," he said into the intercom. The beginnings of a small smile played around the corners of his mouth.

I felt victorious. I'd actually done that. But soon my joy turned to doubt.

Was it right? To purposely manipulate someone's emotions, even if it was, supposedly, for their own good? After all, if Sawyer, or anyone, wanted to be in a nasty mood, did I have the right to decide otherwise? As the implications sank in, I remembered what Star and the others had said about the importance of free will. No, I had no right to do that. I had no right to force my will on an unsuspecting person, no matter how right it seemed to me.

Relax, sis.

I looked down and sure enough my feet floated slightly above the floor. I took a deep breath and immediately touched down, vowing to never manipulate him, or anyone, again.

*The morality thing's complex, huh, Angel? The more
you explore your abilities, the more dilemmas pop up.*

"Let's start with No. 8," Sawyer said to Don, who
began hitting buttons and sliding do-hickeys. Sawyer
turned to speak into the intercom. "We'll start with No. 8
Angel." Of course, he didn't know I could hear everything
outside of the booth.

I nodded and resolved to never manipulate him, or
anyone, again. The music started to play in my headphones.
No. 8 was one of my favorite tracks. Musically, it was
straight pop, but Sawyer had managed to incorporate a
classical cello that captured the mood I was in when I'd
written the lyrics during one of those mind-numbing history
classes. The song was about the uncertainty of a new
journey, and the longing of wanting to share the trip with
someone who understood me. They were my insights right
before The Change happened. I marveled at how far I'd
come since writing them.

Closing my eyes, I put all the emotion stemming from
those revelations into the sounds coming from my mouth.

> *"Is there anyone who understands?"*

I belted the high note and held it, remaining conscious
of the level of intensity and the fact there were mortals
within feet of me.

I continued to hold the note and opened my eyes. The
first and only thing I saw through the window was Sawyer,
and I sang to him:

> *"I know the road is winding/*
> *I know that it's mine alone.*
> *But I know you'll be there to hold my hand/*
> *Until I get back home."*

His eyes bore into me like lasers. The music stopped and the spell was broken. He gestured for me to leave the booth. When I emerged, LaLa and Julietta were all smiles, high-fives, and complimentary pats on the back. Don winked at me before turning back to his soundboard. But Sawyer didn't even deign to look in my direction. I blinked back the red sting of angry tears.

"Julietta, let's do this," he said in a clipped tone.

"I'm not ready," she squeaked. LaLa and I instantly recognized the deer-in-headlights look: Jules was having an anxiety attack. She had them, too, every now and then, especially in situations where she felt inadequate. Despite her lovely voice, she didn't feel capable in this new professional recording environment.

I passed her a hot cup of tea with large squirts of lemon juice and honey. LaLa rubbed her back while whispering an encouraging pep talk. "I'm sorry," Jules said.

"Just give her a few minutes," I told Sawyer and Don.

"We need to take a break anyway," Sawyer said in a monotone. And with that, he left the studio and went outside.

We all looked at each other in confusion. Sawyer never left the studio, especially in the middle of a session. It wasn't my imagination; he was acting bizarre. After making sure Jules was all right, I excused myself, grabbed my knapsack, and went outside, too. It wasn't until I isolated his scent and followed it that I realized I was instinctively tracking him.

His scent led me to his apartment. The door was unlocked, so I walked in. His studio was uncharacteristically dark. I sat in the unlit space and drank down several thermoses while listening to him upstairs, pumping dogged push-ups. After a minute, I made my way up the stairs—something none of us had done since meeting him. The second floor was a long hallway, off of which were a number of closed doors. Each door had a number on it.

Cici picked up on the growing feeling of trepidation I was experiencing. *Angel, what are you doing?*

I had to find him. Intrigued, I followed the strongest trail of his scent, and it led me to one closed door in particular. Number five.

This must be his bedroom, Angel, maybe you shouldn't—

I ignored her and knocked on the door.

"Come in, Angelica," he whispered from behind the closed door. How did he know it was me and why would he think I could hear him whisper? For one second, I considered heeding Cici's warning. But I knew there was no turning back down the hallway. There was no turning back from him. I slowly opened the door.

Sawyer lay, shirtless, on the floor in the middle of his room. On his chest, a thin sheen of perspiration glistened in the muted sunlight fighting its way through heavy black curtains. I stepped inside and closed the door behind me. There was a king-sized bed covered with a mussed black and gold comforter with black sheets. The headboard was a massive antique. A treadmill lived in the opposite corner, and bushy potted trees hinted that sunlight was allowed into the room after all.

And then there was the altar.

His voice was soft. "I can't hide who I am from you anymore."

I was so absorbed in the altar, and the implications, I didn't know he was standing a few inches behind me. "You practice magic." I said in disbelief.

"I'm very much a novice." He paused before continuing. "And…to reference a popular phrase, I see dead people. They've been telling me things. About you. I know you're different."

Panic arose. When I took a deep breath to calm it, the scent of him traveled deeply into my very core. Warning bells set off in my mind. But it wasn't because I was hungry. It was because he was weird like me and I wanted to rejoice. My impulse was to hug him, kiss him. But instead, I fought against the urge until my face felt like stone.

"They won't tell me *why* you're different, though," he continued.

I knew I had to turn around and face him. But my feet seemed glued to the floor.

"Angel. Is this a deal breaker?"

Where was my voice? I couldn't speak.

"If it is, I'd understand." His voice was like velvet behind me. "My mom more or less denounced me because of it." I listened to his footsteps and the subsequent groan of the hardwood floor as he walked back to the middle of the room and sat down. "When I was little...things used to happen around me," he said. "They still do."

I finally turned around to face him. He looked so upset. I wanted to soothe the frown that had again settled on his brow, but I knew if I moved toward him I might not be able to control myself. Knew that if I touched him, I wouldn't, couldn't stop. So I waited. When he continued, it was in a gush, as if he were exhaling after a long moment of holding his breath.

"My parents were both sixteen when I was born. My Dad was an angry, racist alcoholic who hated everybody. He beat her everyday that I can remember."

His Georgian accent came out the more he talked. I was completely enthralled.

"He even beat her when she was pregnant. She lost that baby, and even though I was only four, I knew she lost it because of me. You see, when my parents went at it, I got angry and scared, and things would break. Dad would get injured. And one day, he just disappeared."

"Literally?" He nodded while eyeing me closely.

"I finally told him, 'I wish you would just disappear.' He did."

Whatever he saw on my face made him feel comfortable enough to continue. "The older I got, the more these weird things would happen to the people around me. Like Mom's second husband. He drank *and* did meth. I was nine when he started hitting me. One night he hauled back to punch me again, and just dropped dead. I knew something was really wrong with me when he came to me afterward and thanked me, but no one else could see him."

I wasn't sure which part of Sawyer's story was more disturbing: the abuse, the destructive emotions, his communication with the dead, or that after hearing all of this, I found him even sexier than before.

"Shortly after that, Ma discovered the church. There was a music teacher there who taught music theory and piano. It all helped me feel normal. But the more normal I felt, the more spirits I would see. I had no friends. Instead of going out to play, I shut myself in my room and played my guitar and an old beat-up keyboard the teacher gave me."

I imagined a young, isolated Sawyer, lonely and in his own world of music and unexplained magic. My heart ached for him.

"Eventually, Ma met my step-dad at church. Never treated me bad. But when he found out I was different, she became afraid something would happen to him, too. Said she'd seen it, my way of being, in the family before. Her Mom; my Nana. She begged me not to hurt Mick the way I'd hurt the other two.

"I knew then that I had to visit Nana to understand what I was and what I was capable of. Sophomore year, I got her address and traveled over three counties away. It was the best thing I could have done."

He smiled and my heart melted.

"She told me that when I have strong feelings toward someone—anger, hate, fear, love—it causes magic to happen, sometimes in dangerous ways. Every summer I stayed with her and she taught me how to control my way of being so I wouldn't hurt, or kill, anyone else. Since then, I've worked at it." His hands balled into fists. "I thought it was under control."

I wanted to know more about his grandma, but his tortured eyes stopped my questions. I remained silent and he continued.

"Then I met you. And my world turned upside down. Heist. The shooting at the house. The fights at your concert. People were dying and getting hurt again. And it's because I...have strong feelings for you."

My heart was beating out of control and I wondered if his ever-steady heartbeat was a result of his learned self-control. It was all starting to make sense. His moodiness and his insistence that my getting shot was his fault. All the things he listed were a result of my lack of control, but he'd thought it was his doing. How could I tell him he was wrong? That it wasn't him, that it was actually me? How could I tell him the truth without doing further harm to my family or to him?

Angel, don't you dare...

I'm not going to expose us, Cici. But I have to say something.

I walked over and sat down on the floor in front of him.

"I could never shun you, Sawyer. Anymore than I could shun myself."

We sat there for a while, breathing and exhaling together. Watching each other with cautious, excited eyes. I wondered how intense his "manifestations" were. What would happen to me if he didn't concentrate? The air of danger that always seemed to surround him now made sense. And it made me want him even more. It felt like there had been an unspoken agreement between us that only now was coming to the surface.

"I've always had to hide pieces of me," I continued. "From everyone; people at school, my family, the girls. But I feel like I can tell you anything. As much as I can."

"Your secrets don't define you, Angel. Anymore than mine do."

But don't they? "Things have changed a lot...since we met." I bit my lip.

He reached out and touched my hand. It was like being caressed by a live wire and I quickly pulled away. The smell of him was still intoxicating, but the hunger that was starting to register took a back seat to other sensations. I turned away, unable to face him. "We can't be together, Sawyer. I can hurt you." My voice was so thick I almost didn't recognize it.

"More than I've already hurt you?"

He gently turned me around, and placed a hand on my chin, forcing me to look into his sparkling eyes. "This is dangerous, Sawyer."

"Is it the black/white thing?" His tone was playful, but his eyes were grave as they searched mine. "Boston is full of interracial couples, we won't stick out that much."

I felt the corners of my mouth lift. But the smile quickly died.

His hand was still on my chin. "Your moodiness can be quite dangerous. But I think I can adjust," he murmured. His eyes reached into my soul. I inhaled the sweetness of his breath. But I had to bring this back to reality. And the reality was, despite his revelations of weirdness, he was still mortal. And I was not. In the wake of my Mahá, it was clear I wasn't even a *normal* immortal. At the end of the day, I didn't know *what* I was.

How could I have a relationship with Sawyer when I couldn't be honest about who, and what, I am? How could I put him in constant danger of being killed if I had a moment of weakness? My heart was breaking from the pain of knowing that I had to give up something that I wanted with every fiber of my being.

"I can't. I'm sorry," I said, my voice breaking. I got up and walked out of the room, faster than I should have, but it was the only way to keep going. Because even with the events at my Mahá and the Garden, walking out on Sawyer at that moment was one of the hardest things I'd ever done.

And I finally knew why. I loved him.

I didn't know when it happened. All I knew was that outside of my family, there was no one I wanted to be around more, no one I wanted to know more, no one I thought about more than Sawyer Creed. I shook my head at the irony. Didn't I hate him before I even met him? Now I wanted him on every level imaginable. Including instinctual. One taste of Sawyer would reveal all the music in his head. I would be completely lost in him. And the urge to devour him would overwhelm my reason. I couldn't allow that to happen, even though my very being cried out for it. I had to protect him. From me.

I gave myself time to blink back my tears and strengthen my resolve by slowly walking back to the studio. Once there, I saw Markus had arrived. A group of guys were hanging out in the far corner. All were mortals clad in black denim and goose down. Their pants all hung below their butt cheeks despite the belts. "My crew," Markus said. The guys nodded toward all of us during the informal introduction. All shared that distinct school-of-hard-knocks attitude that many street rappers wear like a badge of honor.

"We're just taking a short break right now," I told Markus.

"I'm ready," Jules said. "Been ready. Is Sawyer coming back soon?" Her tone was loaded.

"Not sure," I said casually. I wanted, needed, to refocus on the work. "Let's practice harmony."

We sang until Sawyer came back a few minutes later. He exchanged fist pounds with the guys and a few quick words with Markus. A covert glance told me he was fully concentrating on the work, too. The unibrow had returned, but there was nothing I could, or would, do about that.

Jules laid down her harmonies. Then I went back in to lay down some filler harmonies. Next up was LaLa. Her lyric delivery had all heads nodding; even Markus' motley crew. Throughout it all, we encouraged and praised each other, but Sawyer kept his back to me. When addressing me he was cold, detached and über-professional.

One of Markus' big hands gently pulled me to the side. "Outside of your Mahá," he said, "we haven't really caught up. Whaddya think?"

As if they had a mind of their own, my eyes automatically slid in Sawyer's direction. All I saw was his back: tense, impenetrable, and...touchable. But, I had to be clear that it could never work between us. I had to stick to my kind, and keep him glamour-free and out of danger. Someday he might understand, but more than likely he would never know that it was all for his own good.

I turned to Markus. "Sure." He smiled back in a benign, friendly way that hid the toothiness.

"Good. Movie and then the Nest?"

"Sounds like fun. Tonight, okay?" He looked doubly pleased. "Come get me," I said before taking a swig from my hot tea. He playfully looked at me sideways and we both laughed. He was the only one in the room who understood the joke of me drinking tea. This was what I needed, I told myself as I giggled a little too loudly. Someone who really got it. Someone who got me.

"You seemed a little perplexed earlier," he whispered. "Are your friends acting strangely?"

"Yes, how did you know?" Surprised, I relayed how LaLa and Julietta seemed to have almost traded roles, although I didn't mention Sawyer's permanent frown, or the reason behind it.

"It's you," he said casually while pushing a stray lock of hair out of my face. "Your newborn energy is affecting the mortals closest to you. Same thing happened to me. I had to lay off hanging out with them so much until I got a little older, more stable."

No one had mentioned this bombshell information to me. Why would I hear it only from him? I asked him as much.

"Your folks don't spend as much time around mortals as we do. Trust me, the longer you're around, the weirder they're gonna get. Someone might even get sick; depends on the person."

As I digested this information, Jackie walked over. "Little Wolf, Sawyer's ready for you now."

Markus disappeared into the booth. There weren't a lot of mainstream rappers that I liked, but he was an exception. His dark lyrics were intelligent and spoke of being an outsider in a world full of pain. His words came across as the truth and now I knew why. There was nothing lonelier than making music with mortals.

As he spit his lyrics, his crew started getting a little rowdy. Jackie came over to tell them to be quiet, but her influence lasted all of two seconds. The noise increased again.

"Y'all need to chill," LaLa said in her strongest alpha-female voice. That squashed the din and even earned a few muted apologies. Markus emerged from the booth to slaps on the back and massive fist pounds from his crew.

"So I'll come to pick you up later, Angel," he said after his boys had already gone. "It's been a while, but I think I remember how to get to your crib."

LaLa and Jules simultaneously gaped at us and then glanced, puzzled, at Sawyer. Markus slid a sly, quicker than mortal look at Sawyer's cutting glance, before offering him his hand. It hung in the air a second too long before Sawyer clapped it fiercely. Markus smiled again, this time full out. I got the impression this rather scary sight was something he rarely afforded mortals. But if he thought the sight of his sharp canines would frighten Sawyer, he was wrong. Unfazed, Sawyer had moved onto the next track as if Markus had already left. Markus, his jaw tight, took his goodbyes from Jules and LaLa and headed out.

The rest of the session went like that, with Sawyer in his own terse little bubble, spitting out orders and keeping everybody on their toes. Musicians, artists, and industry people continued to float in and out of the studio throughout the day. Some came to work, like Joy, who laid down killer bass lines before heading out to a gig later that evening; some who'd heard about the session through the grapevine and came to chill and hang out. Camera phones and camcorders clicked steadily, documenting the occasion.

Eventually, Nina came through to check in on us, and she grew excited when she heard what we'd laid down. "Very nice," she cooed while scrolling through her Blackberry. She dialed. "Listen to this," she said into the phone. "Sawyer, turn it up!"

He complied. The studio took on the ambience of a club: bass thumping, folks dancing. Nina talked excitedly into the phone. LaLa, Jules, and I exchanged round-eyed glances. Nina rarely got passionate over a song.

It felt like moths were flying in the pit of my stomach. "I'm nervous," LaLa said, echoing my thoughts. We hugged, and it was a wordless acknowledgement that our work, the music we had poured our hearts and souls into, made others excited. Jules grinned at the two of us as she went back into the booth to lay harmonies for the next track. Sawyer still frowned.

Eventually, the new moon was high in the sky and we were done. LaLa was uncharacteristically wistful. "Our first real studio recording session comes to a close," she mused. We all hugged again, taking a few last pics to mark the milestone. Don, surrounded by fourteen empty coffee cups, went back outside to smoke what must have been his fifth pack of cigarettes. Nina was marathon-texting in a corner. A few people, including Raj and Jackie, lingered around the studio. Sawyer congratulated us tersely, and then left.

"What did you do to him?" Jules asked as she, LaLa and I made our way outside. Taking note of her confrontational posture, I remembered what Markus told me. What I'd first thought was residual fallout from my Garden-gig improv wasn't that at all. My girls were affected by my change. Sawyer wasn't the only one I'd have to protect from me.

"Sawyer's moody. We knew that going in," was all I said. I sounded as casual as I could while bidding them both goodnight, knowing it would be the last time for a while that we'd spend so much time together. Mom and Dad were right. I had to remove myself from the mortals I loved, and the pain of this truth cut me to the core.

Raj came outside. "Julietta?" he said before taking her hand. They wished us goodnight before climbing into his Benz. How messed up was this? He wasn't even her type. Shocked, I looked to LaLa who just shrugged and giggled.

Seconds later, an Escalade pulled up with one of Markus' boys inside. He opened the car door, and we acknowledged each other with a lift of the chin while LaLa jumped inside. LaLa driving off with a guy she just met was something I never thought I'd see. She waved at me happily through the window as I backed away slowly, head reeling with what I'd just witnessed. The elation of our successful recording session now seemed way in the past as I swallowed tears.

My friends were no longer themselves, and it was because of me.

27. THE FOREVER TYPE

Later, back at home, I glided through the closed front door and heard Cici's laughter tinkling in the family room. Satchel, Markus, Mom, and Dad were in there with her.

Markus rose to his feet. "We've got a half hour before the movie starts," he said while taking my coat. Mom and Dad looked at each other with small smiles.

I sniffed the blood Cici was sipping and my stomach growled. I was so caught up in the energy and rush of the recording session I'd forgotten I'd gone through all the thermoses and hadn't eaten for a while. A long, involuntary hiss emitted from between my lips before I raced to the kitchen and brought back a few goblets.

The doorbell rang. Cici opened the door to find Justin. Mom and Dad discretely retired to another part of the house. Markus eyed Justin like a side of beef, and Cici and Satchel couldn't seem to stop giggling as they went upstairs.

"You haven't eaten for a while, Angel," Justin said, casting an accusing eye on Markus.

My head swiveled between the two of them. Fresh blood was always the best option, but it seemed downright rude to feed with Markus sitting here waiting to get our date started. Justin's blood throbbed in his veins while I regarded the goblet still in my hand...

"Thank you Justin, but we were just about to step out," I said as neutrally as possible. I gestured to the goblet. "I'll be right very soon. No worries."

Justin winced as I quickly downed the contents of the remaining glasses before wiping my mouth with the back of my hand. Markus, seemingly bored, removed lint from his sweater. "Let's go," he said, "before the movie starts."

For a brief second, I wondered what Justin had been doing before he sensed my hunger. He was dressed in black leather pants, black boots, and a mid-length black leather trench, quite a different look from the blue-collar apparel he usually wore. "See you later, Justin?"

"Yeah," he muttered before I closed the door behind him.

Markus reached around to the back of the couch and pulled out two helmets. He offered one to me. "Mind riding my Ducati?"

The sleek, red and black motorcycle, listed by *Rolling Stone* as a favorite in his collection, was illegally parked in front of the house. Fast bikes like that scared the heck out of me, but I wasn't going to let him know that. "Can't wait," I answered, taking the helmet.

He also handed me a shopping bag. "Thought you might like it."

Inside was an Avirex motorcycle jacket; red leather with fleece lining. He held it for me, but I hesitated briefly, wondering if the coat represented a little more than a gift between friends. Deciding to go with the flow and stop over-analyzing everything, I put it on as he nodded with approval.

Later, after the movie (starring one of Markus' rapper-turned-actor colleagues, it was a "drama" that had us laughing in all the wrong places because it was so bad), we lounged in the part of The Nest that was a bar/lounge/nightclub catering to the mortal public. The immortal section, where I had met Justin, was in an area of the building only accessible to folks with immortal DNA or a donor pass. In the midst of mortals and all types of immortals, I sipped from a bottled blood that was kept in a separate section behind the bar and served with a secret code. The bottle looked like a beer bottle; I wondered what would happen if some inebriated mortal accidentally drank from it.

"I remember making little songs with you when we were kids," Markus said, after finishing an extra-rare turkey burger. He placed a leather-clad arm along the back of the couch where we sat. "It felt good working together today."

I had to agree, but the arm made me a little nervous. Did Markus have more than friendship on his mind? I'd just decided to clear the air when a few fans came by to get his autograph. Once word got out about who was behind his sunglasses, a small herd of people stood in line. Markus signed and posed for pictures. "Soon it'll be you," he said to me. I shivered at the thought of being mobbed by groups of people.

After he'd signed about eleven autographs, a big, burly vampire bouncer came to the rescue. He turned the rest away while Markus feigned disappointment. Leery of another potential wave of fans, he suggested we go to the immortal part of The Nest, and I agreed. Moments later, after getting re-situated, I turned to him. "Markus, I really enjoyed our time tonight. But, I don't want to mislead you—"

"Angel, I'm going to stop you right there. I'm gay."

I nearly dropped my bottled blood.

"I'm not ashamed, but I keep it on the DL since that type of press would probably kill my rap career, knowwhatimsaying?"

"Markus," I recovered my composure, "I'll never tell. Your secret's safe."

"Cool. But even if you were my type, I could never get in the way of you and your boy over there." His gaze went over my shoulder. "I could tell earlier you're really into each other."

Expecting to see Justin again, I rolled my eyes before turning around. But it wasn't Justin. It was Sawyer. He was leaning on the bar talking to a girl. I recognized her profile; it was Risa, the seamstress. Her laugh revealed fangs, and she caressed his neck suggestively as if she wanted to use those fangs on him.

Red clouded my vision as my shimshana shivered violently in the pit of my stomach. Instantly, I was at her back, standing before him. His eyes grew wide when he saw me. "He's mine," I seethed before Risa swung around, ready for a fight.

"Angel!" Her usually expressionless face looked shocked as she backed down from my Shimshana heat. The lounge had become deathly quiet. All the eyes of the patrons were on me, and their stares were accompanied by whispers of Risa's impending demise at my hands. Then a waiter hurried over, offered her a donor menu, and that was that.

I took Sawyer by the hand and led him to my family's booth. "What do you think you're doing here?" I demanded.

"Me?" he retorted. "What are *you* doing here?"

"What's going on here?" a third voice asked. It was Justin coming toward us. Fast. I could hear Markus across the room say, "Oh, snap!"

"You're so upset," Justin said to me, "I could feel you."

The two guys in my life eyed each other. "Who the hell is this?" they asked simultaneously.

"Justin, Sawyer. Sawyer, Justin," I said in nervous introduction. When Justin looked at my hand still in Sawyer's, I could feel his despair.

"Excuse us, Sawyer," I said, taking Justin's hand and leading him away to another part of the space. He glanced back at Sawyer, still standing where we'd left him.

"I'd thought something happened with the rapper," he explained. His eyes searched the room until they came to rest on Markus talking to a rough-looking dude with a tattooed face.

"Is that what all this is about?" I shook my head in disbelief. Guys... "Trust me, you don't have to worry about Markus."

Justin pointed a defiant chin at Sawyer. "So you do have a boyfriend."

"It's still none of your business," I said gently not wanting to hurt him further.

"Does he know you, Angel? The way you deserve to be known?" He searched my eyes. After a few seconds, a confident smile spread across his lips. "You're the forever type, Angel. And I'll always be here for you. Forever." He walked away, but his allusion to Sawyer's mortality stayed with me like a troublesome fog as I made my way back to the booth.

But once I returned to Sawyer, the fog and the thought of everything else evaporated as I stood before him, fascinated by his presence. Of all the things Justin said, I chose just one word and let it roll around my head a little.

Boyfriend.

I'd never had one before. Had never felt butterflies flutter alongside quick little fish swimming in my insides. I simultaneously wanted to devour him and protect him. I felt insane. And I loved it. His eyes locked with mine and our fingers intertwined. I marveled at his gorgeous face towering above me, as my fingers itched to pull the elastic from his low ponytail and watch his hair cascade around his square jaw.

"To answer your question," he said referring to our interrupted conversation, "my Nana's immortal. She suggested I come here so I wouldn't feel so alone." Mortals with immortal DNA. That was what Mom had been hinting at. "I came here to find a place to call home. And I found you."

He ran a finger across my cheekbone, and that entire side of my face felt warm and tingly. I had to remind myself there were other people in the room.

But I also told myself that since I knew all about him, it was time he knew all about me. My eyes, half shut from the pleasure of his touch, opened completely as I took his hand in mine and summoned a waiter. "AB," I ordered, "with a splash of O. No ice. Ten, please. And a mineral water." Sawyer's head cocked at a questioning angle and his eyes narrowed as they searched my face. "I'm sorry for walking out of your place like that," I said, stroking the inside of his wrist. "I knew that if I stayed I would end up spilling the beans. Or spilling your blood."

"What...?" The word came out of him as if he suspected there was more, but wasn't sure he wanted to know what it was.

The waiter returned with the glasses of blood. "I wanted to show you who I really am," I picked up one glass. "But I had to protect my family. And I wanted to protect you from me." With that, I downed the glasses at immortal speed. He studied me, then the empty glasses, before turning an astounded stare back to me.

"You're drinking blood," he finally said in a quiet voice. I nodded. He then held my gaze so calmly and completely, I knew there was nothing more I would ever hide from him.

"Eventually, I would have found a way to come back to you," I revealed. "I can't stay away for too long."

"I wanted to get you outta my head and pretend it didn't matter," he said. "But I couldn't. And it does. I can't stay away at all." He smiled as I hovered over the couch. "By the way," he said with a gleam in his eyes. "I was never glamoured. Glamour protection was one of the first things Nana taught me. When you turned away and said 'No, Daddy' it gave me enough time to put the shield up."

I swatted his arm in disbelief. "You knew!"

"I knew your Dad practiced magic, so I figured you did, too and you'd tell me when you were ready. I never thought there was all this." He waved at the empty glasses.

Suddenly, I remembered I was supposed to be on a date with Markus, and that it'd been over a half hour since I'd left him sitting there. Feeling like an awful friend, I excused myself and searched the Nest for him. Nada. Maybe he got lucky with Tattoo Guy. I turned to see Sawyer in front of me, holding up the new bomber jacket as if he'd already done it for me a million times. "I'll take you home," he said with finality, as if there could never be another option. I offered him my shoulders where he placed the jacket before wrapping me in his arms.

28. LOVELY NOTES

Soon Sawyer was bundling me into his sleek, bronze Audi. I commented on the new-car smell.

"Just got it a few days ago. Figured if I was going to be taken seriously, I needed to have a car." His glance suggested he meant being taken seriously by me. I nestled myself into the deep leather seats. Being so close to him in the confines of the car drove me crazy. It took major effort to not grab him and drain him dry. I could do it, faster than anyone who might happen to look through the window could see. He wouldn't even know. But I would know. For eternity.

Sawyer was unaware of the dark thoughts crowding my mind. "Does the heat bother you?" he inquired politely as he pulled into the downtown traffic,

"No. Neither does the cold. My body just adjusts regardless of the temperature."

The dark thoughts continued. One taste of his blood wouldn't satisfy me; I would want more. Much more. I studied his profile. The rise of his nose, the plane of his cheeks. The way the streetlights brought out silvery highlights in his hair. I could never feed from Sawyer. To turn him into a donor would be unfair to him. Unfair to us. And I could never take the chance of losing control with him. I needed him just the way he was. For as long as he was.

His long, pale hands capably handled the steering wheel as he made a curb-hugging turn. Silently, I thanked the heavens that he liked to drive fast. "Angel. What exactly are you?" He threw a knitted-brow glance at me. "Aren't you supposed to have fangs?"

"I don't sleep in a coffin. Or turn into a bat." He chuckled and waited for an answer while I fumbled with the right words. I'd never had to explain what I was before. "I'm immortal. Just like your Nana. There are many types of immortals... I am what's known as Shimshana." I furtively checked his reaction to this. He met my eyes briefly before returning his attention to the road.

"We are the original blood drinkers. We look like everybody else. We don't need fangs. We're warm-blooded and we love the sun. Like everyone else, we feel pain; we get sick, injured, etc. At the Nest, there's lots of blood drinkers, but we all have something in common. We want to, need to, connect fully with our humanity."

"Do all Shimshana sing?"

"Not like me. All immortals have unique abilities of varying degrees."

I sighed and looked out of the window. How much could I tell him without scaring him off? Too much information too soon might push him away and I couldn't bear that now. "My voice can fix things, and hurt people." *Kill people would be more accurate*, I thought. "I can also move really fast, go through solid objects, and freeze time."

I had to give him credit for keeping a steady hand on the wheel. He blinked a few times before composing his face. The alternative rock emitting from the radio was the only sound for an eighth of a mile.

We parked outside of my house. He switched off the ignition and turned to me. His eyes looked wild and they studied me for a long moment. "I know it's a lot," I blurted. "I'll understand if you keep driving away, back to your studio, and refuse to have anything more to do with me outside of music."

He answered by cupping the right side of my face with his hand. He leaned toward me and I felt my lips involuntarily part. His eyes searched mine. "Angel," he breathed seductively, "can I please come inside?" For a few seconds, I forgot where I was. Literally. I actually had to shake my head as if that would help me get back to a normal un-Sawyer-fied state. I then nodded, speechless, before directing him to our parking behind the house.

Dad met us at the door. "Angel," he said sternly, "if you are going to be getting home at this time of night, you should call. Your mom was worried."

"Um, sorry Dad." I prayed he wouldn't ask about Markus.

"I told you both she was okay," Cici said as she and Mom walked down the stairs in slippered feet.

"That's what the lock is for, Abraham," Mom said gently. She looked exhausted, and I felt a pang of guilt for the worry she'd experienced. "Thank you for bringing Angel home, Sawyer," she continued.

"Guess one of them had to," Cici said with a sly grin. I felt my face burn.

"Make yourself at home," Dad said with a grudging tone. "But don't get too comfortable."

Embarrassed beyond reason, I dragged Sawyer away.

"What's the lock?" he asked as we made our way down the hall.

"Cici and Dad are telepaths of a sort. They lock onto my mind in order to monitor and damage control me twenty-four-seven. As a newborn, I'm dangerous, unstable, and can easily kill. I've killed already."

Humiliated, I couldn't even look at his face to see his reaction to my latest bombshell. But he gently lifted my chin and forced me to look into his eyes. They were calm, and fearless. "I know you won't hurt me, Angel."

Did he not hear what I just said? Maybe he had a death wish. "How do you know that, Sawyer?"

"You could've killed me that first day in the studio. I thought you were kissing my neck. You were close, weren't you? But...here I am."

His faith in me released the difficult words that came out in a rush of emotion. "It wasn't you, it was me! I killed Heist. With my voice. He died because he heard me sing!" I lost it then. He took me in his arms as I sobbed with guilt I didn't even know I was still carrying. He stroked my back, methodically, as if he were pulling the stress out of me with his gentle touch. Eventually, I calmed down.

"Your face's a mess," he said gently.

I looked at his once-white shirt. "Your shirt's red, pink, and white."

He wiped away my tears with the ball of his thumb and regarded the red on his finger. "Whoa."

"You still want to stay?"

"Angel, I'm not scared. I've seen some pretty frightening things. Right now I want to hear all about you."

I opened the door to my room and sat on the bed. He pored through my CD collection. "May I?" he asked while holding up my iPod. I tried my best to sound casual, and told him yes, but inside my stomach was in knots. To me, playlists are kind of like the window into one's soul. What if he didn't like my playlists? Or thought my podcasts were boring and my songs juvenile? I bit my lip and pretended I wasn't watching him like a hawk while he read my playlists. He nodded and smiled with pleasure. "I thought I was the only one who listened to this band." He held up the iPod to show me the track. It was a Boston underground rock band with a rabid, local following. Our eyes met, and my stomach relaxed.

I couldn't believe he was standing in my room, and was glad I'd taken the time the day before to pick up the laundry and books previously strewn all over floor. Sawyer softly hummed a tune as he ran his fingers over the bindings of the titles on my bookshelf. I listened to the blood surge through his veins…the hypnotic beat of his heart… I took a deep whiff…mmmm…

"Angel," he was saying. I shook myself out of the daze and focused on his words. "How does it feel? To do what you do?" He came to the bed and sat on the edge, as far away from me as he could. My boyfriend was smart.

"It's still all so new," I answered. "I didn't mature until after I met you."

"Mature?"

I explained the process to him, how a mortal child turns into an immortal adult.

"So the day before you changed was the day Heist died?"

"Yes," I answered with my head bowed in shame.

"It wasn't you. You didn't kill him."

I looked at him, completely puzzled. "How do you know?"

Sawyer's eyes were slightly glazed, and focused on a spot somewhere over my left shoulder. The hair on my arms stood up. "He just told me," he replied. "He's telling me to let you know he just had a bad asthma attack. You weren't the trigger and your voice didn't make it worse. He's been wanting to tell you since that night."

I'd seen some weird stuff in the past weeks, but this took the cake. Even more than angels, ghosts were a complete mystery to me, and I didn't know anyone else who communicated with them. But here I was with Sawyer, talking to Heist's ghost. And his death wasn't my fault. My voice hadn't killed him after all! I imagined Heist's smile and a huge weight lifted off my shoulders.

"We miss you and love you Heist," I said to the air.

Sawyer smiled. "He knows that." He responded to whatever ghostly words he heard and his face grew serious. "Thanks for the heads-up, man." I watched Sawyer's face as his eyes, shining like emeralds witnessed what I couldn't see. I moved to his side and carefully took his hand. Soon I could tell from his facial expression that Heist was gone. I searched his eyes as they slowly refocused on the room. And then on me. Every other sound, every other heartbeat ceased to exist. I heard nothing, and no one, except him.

"I have something to tell you," he whispered. "It's hard for me to feel this way. I have to concentrate even harder. To make sure nothing weird happens. To you. The object of my. Affection."

"I have something to tell you, too," I whispered back as if I was in a confessional. "I got shot because of my own stupidity."

He seemed to turn this fact over in his mind. "I lost control," he said. "That time in the dressing room right before your Garden gig." The memory of the one time I heard his heartbeat speed up confirmed my suspicions. Sawyer's continual concentration was focused on regulating his own heartbeat. I was amazed by the strength of his will.

"When you said everything changed, all I wanted to do was show you how right you were." His fingers caressed mine. "That's why I had to get out of there. As I watched you onstage, how incredible you are, my love took over. I'm sorry for what happened—"

"Sawyer, the audience fights at the Garden. None of that was your fault. It was all me. I know that for a fact."

Relief and joy mixed on his face before it grew serious again. "That may be, Ms. Brown. But it just means I've got to keep doing what I'm doing. Keeping a tight reign on my feelings so that nothing does happen."

The intensity of his feelings and how they might affect me didn't concern me, but I almost wished he would heed this warning of my reckless behavior for his own safety and shun me completely. Yet, a part of me knew it wouldn't matter; something, whether it was one of us or the music, would bring us back together. Still, my baser instincts continued to clash within me. Eat him or love him? The pleasure I would derive from biting him would be overshadowed by the damage done. As Mom said, it would be an unfair advantage. I knew then and there that although I may feel compelled to bite Sawyer, I could not, would not allow it to happen.

"Well, I may be an idiot," he continued, "but I can't imagine not having you around always." He reached out for a lock of my hair. He slowly rubbed it between his fingers before bringing it to his nose. "It's almost unbelievable how nice you smell, Angel." He closed his eyes and deeply inhaled. My heart thumped against my ribs. He rubbed the lock on his face where it mingled with and got slightly caught in his five o'clock shadow. His eyes gleamed with something I'd never seen before, an emotion I couldn't identify but felt down to my very bones, as he slowly caressed the line of my jaw. Through it all, I kept my hands to myself in a supreme effort to keep Sawyer safe.

"I know this is difficult for you, Angel. Heist just told me about your appetite. And your...relationship with Justin. So forgive me, but it's time for you to eat."

"Sawyer, no!" I shrank away from him in horror.

For a second, he was confused by my outburst. Then the light of understanding came on in his eyes. "Silly girl. I'm not offering myself to you. Wait right here, please." He rose and left the room and I marveled over how at home he seemed, as if he belonged in my space. I listened to him as he made his way to the kitchen and started rummaging around the fridge. He hummed the same tune from earlier. The notes were soothing and the colors felt good to my eyes. By the time he came back with a couple pitchers of blood, I was starting to get a little peckish.

"Which one would you like to start with?" His long fingers gestured toward the selections. I pointed at one blindly, ignorant of who it was, only able to keep my eyes locked on him. He poured a glass full, and placed it on the side table at my elbow before returning to his previous seat on the far edge of my bed.

I grabbed the glass and downed it. He shook his head slightly as if to wrap his mind around the flash of movement and the suddenly-empty glass. "Thanks," I said.

"More?"

"Yes, please."

He poured. I drank and we kept our eyes on each other the whole time. A light bulb seemed to go off above his head. "The thermoses you were always drinking from. Blood?"

I nodded while continuing to drink. "It was the only way to not eat all of you." I drank way more than necessary, but it was better to overdo it. I desperately needed to be certain that Sawyer was safe.

"The tune you keep humming, what is it?" I asked.

"I was humming a tune?"

"Yes. Twice. Once in the kitchen, and when you first came into my room."

"I wasn't aware of it," he said with a bemused expression.

Again, we were completely on the same page. He ran out the door and down the stairs. I gave him the head start before sliding through the floor to take a seat at the grand. He ran into the family room and saw me already sitting there. "Cheater," he mumbled before sitting down next to me. His closeness instantly ignited the space between us with electricity.

"I remember every musical arrangement I hear," I revealed to him.

He placed his hands gently on the keys and turned his handsome face to mine. "Then sing it for me, Angel. Sing the tune you've brought out of me." I did. "Again, please Angel," he sang. His voice made my name sound like a caress and thrilled me down to my toes. I sang it again, and this time he accompanied me while his fingers found the right chords. I watched the notes dance before my eyes as he fleshed it out into a sweet ballad.

"That's beautiful," I said in awe. I started to sing a soft counter-melody, no words, just the open-mouthed hum that comes right before you get the lyrics to a new song. When his body began rocking back and forth with the flow of the music, our shoulders touched. The shock of the contact took my breath away. We both stopped. "I can almost see the notes when I'm with you," he said, sounding as awed as I felt.

His hand wandered away from the keys to stroke my ear. I closed my eyes, reveled in his touch, and sensed him lean toward me as his breath grazed my face. I felt like I could die. He leaned in even closer and rested his cheek against the side of my neck before slowly, maddeningly running the tip of his nose from the base of my throat to my ear. I rubbed my cheek against his like a cat rubs against its favorite couch. "You're so warm," he whispered in my ear. "You feel like a Georgian summer."

His voice was husky and rumbly. My heart was beating so fast that for a second I wondered if I was okay. I placed his hand on my heart, and his eyes rounded in amazement at the rapidity of my heartbeat. Removing the rubber band that held his hair back, I slowly ran my fingers through his silky locks. It was his turn to stop breathing for a while as he closed his eyes. I tugged gently, and his eyes flashed open, greener than I'd ever seen them. He frowned with the effort of concentrating so that nothing witchy happened as I took a deep breath; tortured by the delicious smell of him, but sated enough so that my shimshana didn't take over. He drew a little closer and I made up the rest of the short distance until our lips met.

And I heard it clearly…like there was a live orchestra playing in the living room. Music. It was a fragment of a beautiful song in my head. His lips were cool and delicious and moved slowly on mine. There it was…another segment of the song. He kissed the corners of my mouth before nibbling on my lips. The mysterious song fragment continued to play. There was no way anything, anywhere, ever, could compare to this. All I wanted was to be with Sawyer and hear our music until the end of time.

"Angel," Dad bellowed from his workshop. "It's getting later."

Sawyer reluctantly pulled away, but still cupped my face in his large hand.

"Did you hear that too?" he said.

We both smiled then, knowing he wasn't talking about Dad.

# # #

A couple months later, we were all at a swanky Copley Plaza hotel ballroom celebrating Kat Trio's new, real, record deal with Quake.

" 'No. 8, featuring Little Wolf' " is on track to go number one in download sales this week," Nina announced into a microphone as we all raised glasses and applause broke out around the room. Due to an online press juggernaut, the track became a hit on Internet radio and went viral before we had time to title it; so "No. 8" stuck.

Mom, Dad, and Mr. C. gave me big hugs. "Told you you were a star," Cici said, looking stunning in a black cocktail dress and dramatic eye makeup. Earlier, she'd applied her skills to my eyes to make them look sultry and mysterious, too, but now she shook her head at the designer jeans I'd chosen to put on. *At least you're wearing makeup and heels.* She gave us all hugs before she walked off with Satchel. I turned to the girls.

"Why's Raj staring at you like that?" LaLa asked Julietta. We all looked at him while pretending not to, and sure enough, he was watching Jules with sad puppy-dog eyes. We turned back to each other and laughed hysterically.

"Another heart broken by Julietta Hernandez," I said in a radio announcer tone.

LaLa waved to Fearmonger, who was across the room talking to Markus and the crew. Both rappers raised their chins and flashed peace signs. "He acts so hard in public," LaLa confided, still looking at Fearmonger, "but when we're alone, he's a big teddy bear."

Jules and I exchanged happy, amazed smiles. Who'd a thunk?

They looked at me expectantly, waiting for the dish. "Sawyer's new crib is coming along," I offered. "Still not a lot of furniture, but his studio's almost done."

"Wow," Jules said, "So cool he ended up buying the house you were shot in."

"He told me it was in that house, kneeling by my side, post-gunshot, that he fell in love with me."

"Awwww…" they crooned simultaneously.

"I know!" It was exciting to be sharing with my girls again. "It's more homey than his apartment was, and he combined the living room and formal dining room. Now there's two grand pianos in there. One for him and one for me."

"Wow, he's teaching you how to play." LaLa's head bobbed up and down in simple approval.

"So awesome," Jules added with a knowing nod.

Sawyer and I were working to finish the song from the day of our first kiss, but since we could only hear it when our lips met, we weren't in much of a hurry to stop long enough to work it out. In the meantime, we wrote other songs, played for and sang to each other, and insulated ourselves in a world of music. He was the only mortal I spent a lot of time with, and, luckily, he was okay; my presence didn't affect him.

I caught sight of Justin across the room and felt a fleeting pang of loss. Sawyer made sure I was constantly sated with stored blood, and as a result, I hadn't seen my eternal donor since the night at the Nest. After a long pause and a quick, sad smile, Justin turned his back to me and resumed talking to a curvy redhead in a blue mini skirt.

Sawyer made his way over to me through a sea of handshakes and pats on the back. "Congratulations, Kat Trio!" he told us all before looking into my eyes. "It looks like your dreams are coming true."

With a smile and a wave, LaLa and Julietta left us alone.

"My dream is definitely coming true," I said, taking his hands in mine. He was my boyfriend, and the sounds of our celebrating family, friends, and colleagues faded away until his voice, breath, and heartbeat was all I heard.

"Mine too," he whispered before kissing me, softly, in front of everyone. Our secret music began to play…

Take it easy, sis.

I ignored Cici's warning and instead promised myself to love him with no hesitation. One day Sawyer would die. But until then, his heartbeat would be my song in a major key. And while music existed without him, there were no lovely notes without Sawyer.

The record deal and Sawyer. Mom and Dad said it was all fleeting. But I had built my new world on that which is fleeting. And I was willing to pay the price.

THE END

Acknowledgements

So many souls have helped get this book out into the world. First and foremost I thank Papa, Grace and all those others who paved the way. Thank you Eshu, Oshun, Shango, Oya and Obatala.

Thanks to my brother Jeff for helping when no one else would. Thank you Boston Public Library for being the shelter in the storm where I could write. Thank you to my personal angels: Burrell, Anestine, Alimi, Michael T., Nina, and my father Hal. Many thanks to Baba Adeyemi for helping me find the Light in the darkest of days. Thank you Elaina for being this book's first fan and encouraging me to stay the course.

Most of all I thank my child for unconditional love and support through all the sunny afternoons that found mommy typing away at the laptop instead of going to the park. You are my reason for being. You are my heart. You are my all.

Blood To Blood

Dear Reader:

Thank you for reading *Blood To Blood*. If you liked what you read, please take a few minutes to leave a quick review on Amazon.com or Goodreads, and don't forget to tell your family and friends.

Also look out for the sequel, *Heart To Heart*, in Spring/Summer 2014, as well as the first book in a new series based on Justin McCarthy called *To Protect and Serve*, also scheduled for release in 2014.